GUNFIGHTERS IN HELL

OTHER FIVE STAR WESTERNS
BY MAX BRAND:

In the Hills of Monterey (1998); *The Lost Valley* (1998); *Chinook* (1998); *The Gauntlet* (1998); *The Survival of Juan Oro* (1999); *Stolen Gold* (1999); *The Geraldi Trail* (1999); *Timber Line* (1999); *The Gold Trail* (1999); *Gunman's Goal* (2000); *The Overland Kid* (2000); *The Masterman* (2000); *The Outlaw Redeemer* (2000); *The Peril Trek* (2000); *The Bright Face of Danger* (2000); *Don Diablo* (2001); *The Welding Quirt* (2001); *The Tyrant* (2001); *The House of Gold* (2001); *The Lone Rider* (2002); *Crusader* (2002); *Smoking Guns* (2002); *Jokers Extra Wild* (2002); *Flaming Fortune* (2003); *Blue Kingdom* (2003); *The Runaways* (2003); *Peter Blue* (2003); *The Golden Cat* (2004); *The Range Finder* (2004); *Mountain Storms* (2004); *Hawks and Eagles* (2004); *Trouble's Messenger* (2005); *Bad Man's Gulch* (2005); *Twisted Bars* (2005); *The Crystal Game* (2005); *Dogs of the Captain* (2006); *Red Rock's Secret* (2006); *Wheel of Fortune* (2006); *Treasure Well* (2006); *Acres of Unrest* (2007); *Rifle Pass* (2007); *Melody and Cordoba* (2007); *Outlaws From Afar* (2007); *Rancher's Legacy* (2008); *The Good Badman* (2008); *Love of Danger* (2008); *Nine Lives* (2008); *Silver Trail* (2009); *The Quest* (2009); *Mountain Made* (2009); *Black Thunder* (2009); *Iron Dust* (2010); *The Black Muldoon* (2010); *The Lightning Runner* (2010); *Legend of the Golden Coyote* (2010); *Sky Blue* (2011); *Outcast Breed* (2011); *Train's Trust* (2011); *The Red Well* (2011); *Son of an Outlaw* (2012); *Lightning of Gold* (2012); *Comanche* (2012)

GUNFIGHTERS IN HELL

A WESTERN TRIO

MAX BRAND®

FIVE STAR

A part of Gale, Cengage Learning

GALE
CENGAGE Learning·

Detroit • New York • San Francisco • New Haven, Conn • Waterville, Maine • London

GALE
CENGAGE Learning·

LIBRARY OF CONGRESS CATALOGING-IN-PUBLICATION DATA

Brand, Max, 1892–1944.
   Gunfighters in hell : a western trio / by Max Brand. — 1st. ed.
     p. cm.
   ISBN 978-1-4328-2604-8 (hardcover) — ISBN 1-4328-2604-2
(hardcover)
   I. Title.
PS3511.A87G794 2012
813'.52—dc23   2012028646

First Edition. First Printing: December 2012.
Published in conjunction with Golden West Literary Agency.
Find us on Facebook—https://www.facebook.com/FiveStarCengage
Visit our website—http://www.gale.cengage.com/fivestar/
Contact Five Star™ Publishing at FiveStar@cengage.com

Printed in Mexico
1 2 3 4 5 6 7 16 15 14 13 12

ADDITIONAL COPYRIGHT INFORMATION

CONTENTS

GUNLESS GUNMAN 9

THE FIGHTING COWARD 71

GUNFIGHTERS IN HELL 135

★ ★ ★ ★ ★

Gunless Gunman

★ ★ ★ ★ ★

In 1934 seven of the eight stories that Frederick Faust contributed to Popular Publications' *Star Western* were published. "Gunless Gunman" was the fifth story, appearing in the September issue. The story was published under Faust's Max Brand byline. In this pursuit story, gunman Tom Dallas finds himself to be both the pursued and the pursuer, a circumstance that leads him into the midst of the lion's den, without the use of his gun. This is the story's first appearance since its original publication.

I

Tom Dallas was born on the 1st of January five minutes before midnight, just too late, as his friends used to say, for Tom to make any good resolutions. So he lived without them for twenty-two years.

He was big, lazy, graceful; he had night black hair and blue eyes in which the devil from time to time kicked up his heels—a devil that always wore spurs.

On his twenty-second birthday, just before midnight of the 1st of January, certain things conspired to make Tom Dallas decide to change his way of living. The things that conspired were three or four sheriffs who wanted his hide together with three or four score of personal enemies who he had collected in his brisk young life. In addition, on this 1st of January just before midnight, a man lay on a barroom floor with a growing patch of red on his chest and a certain vacant smile in his eyes that Dallas had seen before. The fellow had made two mistakes. One was in dealing himself aces off the bottom of the pack and the other was in drawing two old-style Navy model Colts to enforce his dealing system. But though the killing was certainly justified, a certain "decent respect for the opinion of mankind" led Dallas to the conclusion that things were getting pretty hot in that neighborhood.

All the other killings had been justified, too. They had just had to happen. But, nevertheless, there was this group of sheriffs and individuals who wanted the scalp of Dallas. They wanted it so badly that, as he looked down at the dead man, the hair seemed to rise lightly on his own head.

So, while the gun was still warm in his hand, he unloaded it and made—almost at the twenty-second anniversary of the moment of his birth—a vow that he would not pack bullets in his old bone-handled .45 for an entire year. That done, he slung the empty gun under the pit of his left arm and felt that his conscience had been lightened. You might have asked why he carried the gun at all, and to this he would have replied, with his delightful smile, that that gun was his oldest friend in this world.

Considering the environment in which Dallas lived, no gambler would have bet a ten spot on his existing more than a few days after that gun of his was not loaded, but Dallas continued right through the year to the 2nd of July before the serious trouble overtook him. Of course there had been brawls during that interim, but the old gun, empty as it was, had seen him through.

He had learned to throw it with the accuracy of an Indian's tomahawk and with results almost as deadly. Or if it delivered only a glancing blow, he was immediately behind it, exploding his hundred and ninety pounds of whalebone and dynamite behind two sets of case-hardened knuckles. So, in the long course of six months—equal to sixty years of your life or of mine—he had collected no more than a shallow knife cut across the ribs and a bullet hole through his low-crowned sombrero that pleasantly increased the ventilation during the hot weather.

Then came the 2nd of July.

The thing happened without any malice aforethought on his part. In fact, Dallas never had looked for a fight in his life; he simply found them by chance.

He had stopped along the winding mountain trail, hemmed by lodgepole pine and huge boulders, at a little combination store, hotel, and saloon set up on high stilts over the mountain slope. He sat his horse, looking down off the edge of the cañon that opened onto the level of the desert, and, through the purple haze of desert dust, glimpsed an occasional glitter of a window from the miniature shacks of Spring Water crouching somnolently below, under the shelter of the mountain.

Tom Dallas intended to go on to Spring Water, but not for the sake of the spring, which was an alkali well. He could not have told you why he wanted to go to Spring Water except for something that he had seen once when he had gone through that town with a mob behind him, as noisy as a train of tin cans behind the tail of a dog.

It was then that he had looked aside through the cloud of his own dust and seen a girl with that Mexican bloom of darkness in her face and that sprinkling of Mexican stardust in her eyes. She had been standing beside the street with a market basket over her arm. He did not know where she lived; he was not at all sure that he would recognize her again, because in that infinitesimal instant she had been to him a leap of the heart rather than a detailed picture. Yet Dallas was traveling three hundred miles in order to find her again.

Such profound considerations, such wise impulses were behind all the actions of his life. Not that women bulked very large on his horizon. He might have been making this trip if the beauty he had seen in Spring Water had been an outstanding horse with the right kind of hellfire in the eye.

He looked down at his own horse that, having had a drink at the creek, was now greedily at work on some crushed barley in a nose bag, stamping, snorting, switching its tail, and wriggling its body with hungry delight. It was a good sort of a horse. Tom Dallas had enjoyed owning it for all of eight days but, like everything else he had ever possessed, his pleasure in it was gone.

It was just a horse—and not *the* horse. He had been in many towns, but never in *the* place; he had looked with joy on a thousand mountains, but *the* mountain had never glorified his eye; he had smiled on a hundred girls, but *the* girl had never appeared.

He was eating sandwiches of stale bread and hard cheese, his jaws aching a little as he munched, but the bottle of beer was really well chilled in the water of the creek. A young woman had brought it to him.

She must have been almost pure-blooded Indian, her cheek bones, mouth, and jaw were so heavy. The last of her girlhood, the final gleam of a wild grace was dying out of her eyes that were beginning to pucker in the corners. Dallas thought not of her but of that satin brightness of softness. *The* woman would have that. She would be proud, but never rude, deathlessly faithful, informed but innocent, about five-feet-six inches tall, weight a hundred and twenty pounds, eyes, blue—cornflower blue—, hair not golden, which is too flashy and fades badly, but the sort of brown that turns golden in the sunlight, and, finally, age—well, about eighteen or nineteen or twenty, or something like that. Just the right age. He would know it when he saw it.

Comparing this ideal woman with the swarthy beauty who drew him back to Spring Water, he wondered why he was making the trip.

He had reached this point in his reflections when the squaw brought him another bottle of beer, unasked. He took it with the smile and the quick shine of the eyes that always showed his pleasure. And she was opening the cap and letting some of the cool foam run down the side of the bottle, when he saw something else in the back of his head, rather than from the corner of his eye.

It was not a shape. It was the old ghostly gleam of danger to which he was far more sensitive than any film is to light. The turn of his head showed him a tall man with a bulging forehead and a sallow, concave face ornamented with a pair of drooping mustaches, stepping from the door of the bar. He wore spurred boots on his feet and his right palm was clenched about the butt of a blue-steel revolver that he was leveling at Dallas.

Tom Dallas spun sidewise from the saddle and landed on his knees with one hand on the earth before the little porch of the saloon. From the other hand, as a bullet whizzed over his head, he hurled his empty gun into the face of the stranger.

From hands and feet, Dallas sprang up in time to avoid the bottle that the squaw had swung with a hearty intent of braining him.

The tall man was staggering back with his hands thrown out in a vain effort to regain his balance. He must have made half a dozen of these quick backward steps before he fell over the end of the porch.

The time between his disappearance and the sound of his fall—the flopping noise of loose flesh against the ground—showed the distance he had dropped. The squaw ran with the speed of a boy down the steps and around the corner of the porch.

When Dallas picked up his empty gun and stepped to the edge of the verandah, he saw, far below, the other man stretched flat on his back with eyes half open and a sick smile on his mouth.

Dallas made a little hissing sound through his teeth. He knew what those half-opened eyes and that smile meant. They meant the end. The man's neck had been broken by the fall.

The squaw was pushing back the flap of the man's coat and pulling out a wallet. She took money out of this and shoved it into a pocket of her apron. After this she took a big jackknife out of the trousers of the dead man. She opened the long blade, looked at the edge of it. Was she going to make a good-Indian gesture and put an end to herself?

"Hey . . . look out!" shouted Dallas.

She looked up at him with calm, disinterested eyes, seized a mass of her loose hair, and began to saw it off. She went on chopping off masses of that black hair until the short remainder tumbled without direction. She withdrew herself to the wreck of a buggy that leaned with broken wheels against a tree. Into the seat of the old rig she climbed and, sitting there, began to rock herself back and forth and utter long, weird screams.

She looked like a child playing horse, driving an imaginary journey, but Dallas knew that this was a journey to hell with the soul of her man.

Dallas looked down again to the dead face. Had he known that man before? No, it had been another of a similar aspect—a fellow with a nose not so concave, with a forehead not quite so bulging, with mustaches of the same sandy color, but neatly trimmed. Or perhaps there had been no one at all; perhaps it was only a trick of his imagination. Nevertheless, a vague sense of trouble persisted in the mind of Dallas.

He called to the woman on the seat of the buggy, demanding to know what he could do, and to whom he could send a message about what had happened.

She answered only with continued howling. She would go about things in her own way, have her fill of noisy mourning, then perhaps call in a neighbor or two, and bury her man— husband or not.

If Dallas remained, he would do no good and get nothing but a knife in the back.

He took out his money, counted out $520, left $260 of this weighted down by the empty beer bottle, finished his glass of beer, and went down to his horse.

II

Tom Dallas carried with him a notebook that contained all the records of his active life. The notebook was very small and the life had been very crowded, yet only half of the pages had been filled.

To a chance reader the book would have meant little. Under the heading of July 2nd, for instance, he had jotted down:

Cold beer—dishface—backsteps—Indian song—$260.

This short notation would call to the mind of the writer, however, the excellence of the beer he had been drinking—the peculiar conformation of the face of the man who had come gunning for him—the staggering backward steps of the same individual—the lament of the squaw—and finally the cash price of the affair.

Under the heading of July 3rd came the following:

Dishface Jerry Richmond—faro spurs—greaser blank.

Enlarged, this meant that he had arrived in the town of Spring Water on the afternoon of July 2nd, and that on the next day he had received information that the dead man was one Jerry Richmond—that he had played faro and lost every possession down to his spurs—that he had searched the town for the Mexican beauty of his memory and had been quite unable to find her.

In fact, he was so disgusted by this bad luck that he would have left the town at once except that he lacked the means of paying his hotel bill. So he pawned his spurs and went back to the faro table on the morning of the glorious 4th. At noon he had $1,000; at 3:00 P.M. he had 25¢; at 7:00 P.M. he had quit with $800 in his pocket after buying several rounds of drinks for the entire house.

He did not quit because he was tired of the game. He would have remained at it all that night and all the next day except that the train of his thoughts was broken. For a man with sun-faded eyebrows and sun-faded eyes said at his elbow: "Did you know Jerry Richmond?"

Dallas frowned absently, and then nodded. It was a matter of pride with him that he knew the names of his dead.

"D'you know his brother, too?" asked the fellow with the faded eyes.

"No."

"Sam Richmond is his name," said the other, and smiled a faint malicious smile.

Dallas frowned. Sam Richmond was a name that meant something ominous, but his memory was a little cloudy on the point because he was not a fellow to take other men too seriously.

He went to the bar, had a drink, and said in a noncommittal voice: "Sam Richmond is *muy diablo,* eh?"

The fellow next to him jerked his head around and stared. "Are you askin' or statin?" demanded the stranger.

"I was asking," said Dallas, smiling. "I've been hearing some talk about him."

"You're right," said the other. "When it comes to guns, he's smoother than the lick of a dog's tongue."

The bartender had overheard. "Fifteen is Sam's count, ain't it?" he asked gently.

That was enough to satisfy Dallas.

He went out into the street convinced that the one sensible thing for him to do was to leave Spring Water at once. The sandy-haired gent had been conveying a slightly malicious but very useful warning to him that, elaborated to the full, simply meant that he had been identified as the slayer of Jerry

Richmond. And that another man—that famous brother of the dead Jerry—would now rush along his trail of vengeance, find him, and kill him if he could.

This thought brought Dallas as far as the stables behind the hotel, but when he was in the act of saddling his horse, he paused. He never had run away in his entire life. And if he simply bought a bit of .45-caliber lead for that old gun. . . . But here he remembered that he had vowed not to load that gun— not for another six months, at least.

He swore to himself, and his eyes were clouded with trouble. To run away was disgusting. Not to run was madness. And yet he had an overpowering desire to see the great Sam Richmond and learn if he was, in fact, the remembered fellow with the slightly concave face and the neatly trimmed mustaches.

Dallas went out on the street to think. By this time the sun was down, the fire rimming the horizon was turning to smoke, and a cooling wind had commenced to blow from the mountains. There was still an occasional loud explosion of firecrackers sometimes followed by the shrill yelling of children or by the sudden howl of a dog. Music of a band sounded from the plaza in the center of the town.

Dallas built a cigarette and lit it. "I'm going to get out of here," he told himself, aloud. "I wouldn't be fool enough to stay."

But with that resolution still printed in the frown of his brow, he found himself walking down the street. Perhaps it was the music that was drawing him.

He turned into the old plaza. A dance floor of a kind had been laid in the middle of the square. The band played near it. In front of the three little restaurants that faced the plaza tables had been placed where food and drinks were being served. Dallas slipped suddenly into a chair at one of these tables. He had recognized in his blood the old thrill of ice, and in his brain the old cloud of fire that went hand in hand with the temptation of danger.

Could he resist it now?

Music and liquor, and the stars in the sky, and the girls who were pretty enough, but the one face of perfect beauty that he had ever seen was—danger. He tried to be logical. For six months he had bluffed his way through various troubles. He had handled tough situations one after the other. But Sam Richmond was another matter. An empty Colt thrown at his head would not be enough for Sam Richmond. A bullet from his gun would split the wishbone of the fool who tried such clownish tactics.

And yet Dallas knew that he had to stay. It was throwing himself off the edge of a cliff—but nevertheless he would stay. He had yielded to the thrilling temptation too many times, and now he had no cold blood left in him. The mere thought of Sam Richmond was a spark, and he was all dry powder.

To load his Colt—no, there was a vow against that. Besides, the whole glory of joy would be in waiting with empty hands, and then seeing what happened. As he wiped the cold sweat from his face with his bandanna, he saw the girl for the first time.

She wore tan-colored riding clothes and a wide-brimmed hat. A ray of light showed that she had luminous brown hair. She was about five feet six. He guessed her weight at exactly a hundred and twenty pounds.

Certainly she would have blue eyes. . . .

All at once Sam Richmond was forgotten, and the music began to have a new and rich meaning. He could feel it under his ribs and in his knees.

She went through the crowd slowly, as though she were searching for someone, and there were plenty of men who were willing to be found. Three or four in succession stopped her, spoke, and then something about her made them stop grinning and step back.

Suddenly Dallas was walking behind her.

She was about five feet six, measured against the height of his shoulder, and she stepped exactly as she ought to. Men should be made of whalebone and dynamite. Women should be made of midnight blue and stardust and fine watch springs. This girl was made of these things. He could perceive it even when her back was turned.

So he trailed her, keeping just behind, and watched her look earnestly into the face of one man after another. Each man who was so scanned was sure to turn sharply toward her and speak— but every one of them stepped back again at the first shake of her head.

That was queer. It was so queer that it amounted to a mystery. For it was not exactly the place or the time for a girl to be wandering around alone. And there were plenty of men here lighted with alcohol so that they could see their way clearly into any sort of deviltry.

Then Dallas struck on an explanation. It was shockingly simple. Of course these men simply saw in her face some frightful blemish, some horrible pock-marking of a disease, or the ghastly distortion of a scar.

A Mexican, big, glittering with silver *conchos,* very drunk, lurched toward the girl but halted at the last moment when he was almost careening into her, and swept on his hat as he staggered back again.

And as the girl shrank from him, she saw big Tom Dallas stopping behind her and whirled suddenly toward him.

"Can I help you hunt?" he asked. "Can I . . . ?"

He leaned a little closer, and then felt the shock that had made other men recoil. She had the blue-eyed beauty of a child, the exquisite and perfect innocence that unnerved the hardiest of men.

He understood perfectly. A fellow who wanted a rousing evening would as soon think of plucking an angel out of heaven for a partner as of sitting down with this girl.

But there was where the difference lay. Tom Dallas did not want a rousing evening. He had quite enough of a rouse when his mind touched on the thought of the coming of the great Sam Richmond. But here, under his eyes, placed before him by a divine chance, was that girl of his innermost conception. *The* girl.

She improved upon the most detailed imagination. For who would have thought that a smile slightly crooked and a dimple in one cheek made, of all smiles, the only perfect one? But, in the living flesh, she proved that this was the truth.

"You *will* help me?" she asked.

"I've been sitting over there for hours and hours . . . for all my life, practically," said Tom Dallas, "waiting for nothing except a chance to be a little helpful to you."

III

She was so extremely pleased and happy to be with him that it made not the slightest difference where they sat. She said so.

He found a table back under an adobe arcade and got a Mexican waiter. "You watch this table, understand?" said Dallas.

"Yes, *señor*. I have many tables to watch, and. . . ."

"You only have one table. That's it. If I lift a finger, you'll be at hand." He passed a bill into the hand of the Mexican and the brown face shone like a dark star.

The girl sat with her wrists on the edge of the table and her fingers interlaced, while she smiled at Dallas.

Beer was brought at once. A good swallow of it helped him out of his mental dizziness by the familiarity of the taste and the refreshing coldness. But still it was like sitting in a dream, the very one that he had seen on many a day along many a dreary mountain trail with the head of his black horse nodding before him.

Then he heard her saying: "You're thinking very hard about something."

He looked down at her hands. He had never been able to picture the hands of his ideal. Perhaps he had not even thought of them. But these, he could see instantly, were perfect.

"You're twenty years old?" he asked. "And you weigh about . . . one hundred and twenty?"

"I'll be twenty next month," she said. "Is that the way you guess everything?"

"Well," said Dallas, "I'm just thinking how lucky that I ran into you. . . ."

"How queer," said the girl. "Then it wasn't chance at all. You knew that I wanted you?"

"Wanted me? I knew you wanted someone. I only hoped. . . ."

She sipped her beer. No one else in the world had ever tasted beer in that manner, with that delicacy. Afterward she smiled up at him. He could see that her manners were as perfect as her beauty and her beauty was as perfect as heaven.

"But now . . . when I think . . . I know that not even you could help me. No one could." The girl sighed.

"No one?" he repeated. "Why not?"

"Because it's all so strange. People don't . . . they don't like strange things," she said. "Or places."

"Don't they?" asked Dallas. "That's where I'm different from the rest, then."

"You *are* different from the others, aren't you?" said the girl.

"Well, in spots, maybe. My name is Tom Dallas. What's yours?"

"Sally Jones."

It was not a common-sounding name. It was delightful. It was not like any other name in the world. Any other possible name for her would be too fancy, but Sally Jones was just right. It was as right as her eyes or her smile. And nothing could be righter than those.

"There's something troubling you," he said. "I knew, the moment I looked at you, that there was some sort of trouble."

"How wonderful of you," said Sally Jones. "How could you tell?"

He felt such pride that it choked him for a moment. "I don't know," he said at last, "I just knew." He lifted his finger.

The waiter brought more beer.

"But I haven't finished the first glass," said the girl.

"Fresh . . . you ought to have it fresh and cold," said Dallas.

"If I told you what my trouble really is . . . no, I never could tell anyone that," said the girl. "I could only tell where I have to go. Did you ever hear of Los Gatos?"

"In California?" he asked.

"No. In Mexico."

Los Gatos? Could he tell where it was? Yes, he could tell all about it. And Los Gatos could tell a great deal about him. It knew a lot about him and it wanted to know a lot more. It wanted to have him in the *juzgado* for prolonged study, in fact. All because, after one evening he spent in the town, the mayor and the police had dared him to come back for a second party. And he had come back for the second party.

When he thought of Los Gatos, it was like thinking of a red-hot place on the top of a stove. All Mexico was fairly warm as far as he was concerned. But Los Gatos was filled with men to whom he would be a deathless memory. When he thought of the town he could almost hear the gritting of teeth, the spat of bullets against an adobe wall next to his head.

"Los Gatos in Mexico? Yes, I know where it is," he said softly.

"Do you? How really wonderful," said the girl.

And she adored him, almost too openly, with her head held a little to one side. A look like that, well, it meant heaven—and sharp knives, too—in certain parts of the world. In Los Gatos, for instance.

"That's where I have to go," she said slowly. "But I can't go alone. I have to go invisibly. You know . . . not a soul must dream where I am, and I must appear again in Los Gatos. And that's why I . . . no, I don't dare to ask you."

He took a firm grip upon himself and made his voice calm. The effort made the blood beat in his temple. "Do you want me to take you to Los Gatos?" he asked.

"I didn't dare to . . . ," she began.

"I'd take you to the hottest town in hell," said Dallas. Then he stammered: "I . . . I didn't mean. . . ."

But she was only laughing. "Never mind. I like the way you said that. And I understand. . . ."

It was apparent that he could do or say no wrong. The girl had placed her trust in him. And that trust was like the faith of an angel.

Well, he smiled grimly, after he once showed his face in Los Gatos, only the angels would be likely to enjoy his company. But then, inspired, he saw that this was the price. There is never something for nothing in this world. That flood of innocent faith and confidence that was pouring from her to him—he had to pay for it. And the price was Los Gatos.

"There's only one thing to find out," he said. "When do we start?"

"Do you mean that you're ready? How can I thank you," said the girl.

"Whenever you say."

"Now!" she cried.

"Now? Right now in the dark of the night?"

"Oh, no. Not till you've finished your beer," she said.

He cleared his throat. "I'd like to ask why you're so burned up about getting to Los Gatos," he said.

"I wish that I could tell you," said the girl.

"Something mighty important, of course."

"The life of a man. . . ."

"Ah?" said Dallas. And all the joy went out of him. There was a man. Of course there was a man. The sound of her voice, alone, would be enough to bring millions of men as honey brings flies.

"An American?" he asked. And when she said—"Yes."—he said: "What's he like?"

"Well, let me see," she answered, studying her hands. "Well, rather like you. So like you"—her enthusiasm came bubbling like music into her voice again—"that the moment I saw you I knew I could give you my whole trust."

He took a deep breath. So it was like that. For another man he was to take the trip to Los Gatos. For another man he was to face the Mexican knives and bullets. All for an infernal scoundrel, no doubt—a rascal who had deserted her and who she had to pursue, carrying her poor, slighted heart in her hand.

"Your husband . . . this other fellow?" he asked as gently as possible.

"Oh, no."

"But he will be, one day?"

The girl murmured something. He couldn't hear what. And he did not ask.

"We'll have to chart the course. The towns we're to go through, and all that," he said.

"The towns? But I mustn't go through any towns!" she exclaimed. "I have to disappear . . . don't you see? Never be seen till I'm in Los Gatos!"

"You mean," repeated Dallas in a daze, "that you and I . . .

alone, through the mountains? You mean we travel alone and . . . Los Gatos . . . ?"

She broke into this staggered mumbling to say: "Isn't that the beauty of it? They never will dream of looking for me in the mountains and the desert."

"No," gasped Dallas. "I . . . I don't suppose they will. And . . . we're starting now?"

"Oh, not if you don't want to go? Or are you a little ill, Tom? You seem quite drawn."

He leaned his hands on the table, prepared to rise. It was not a dream. She was there, opposite him. Her voice had just finished making music. And they were going to Los Gatos . . . alone.

IV

He could see the lights of Los Gatos scattered in the valley beneath the bare mountainside. Even those lights were different from the gleam that an American town throws into the wide night. They were dimmer, more yellow, with somehow a sinister, unfriendly tremor about them.

Sally Jones had finished scrubbing up the pans. She had acted as cook and bottle washer all through these days, and a very good cook and very neat bottle washer she had proved. She was surprising. She was surprising in a lot of ways.

For instance, he had added to the pack for the trip a neat Winchester that he could not use even on game because the terms of his inward vow were that he was to have no loaded weapon in his hands for six months. But the rifle might be a protection to the girl better than his pair of hands. And this morning, as they rounded a shoulder of a hill, a deer had sprung away like the wind. She had slicked the rifle from the saddle holster and snapped it to her shoulder. Only for an instant the muzzle of the rifle swung to follow the flight of the deer. Then the gun barked and the deer fell.

"What luck!" Sally Jones had cried.

But from the first movement to the last, he had recognized it for what it was—skill—sheer skill.

A girl who likes her beer and shoots deer on the run—there was something besides stardust and blue skies in her.

And then when a whirlpool of dust was caught up into the wind right under the nose of her horse, the third day out, and the bang-tail had begun to buck like a fiend, she had sat out that frantic pitching like an old stager, and laughed, and her eyes were shining at the end. "Poor little old pinto," she said. "He was just having a dull trip for himself."

She kept on laughing for a while, and her eyes held a brighter light for hours afterward.

She was an orphan, a fact that made him pity her with a swelling heart but that was a relief as well, because it meant that two people were not in an agony of worry about her. He could not learn very much about her past, or the situation from which she had come.

"If I tell you that, I'll be telling you the secret, and it really isn't my secret to tell, Tom," she would answer.

So he closed his teeth and stared bleakly into the blue distance ahead. After all, a girl who can ride a bucking bronco and shoot deer at three hundred yards on the run and who is also a boss camp cook. . . .

Well, there were other things to put against these.

When the mountain thunderstorm swept roaring down the cañon that night, she had been frightened, and even when she cuddled up close to him and he put a big arm around her, every rip of lightning and every blast of thunder sent a shudder through her. He liked to remember that moment.

Also, when she ran a sliver into her finger, she had come to him with great eyes and turned her head sharply away while he carefully dug the thorn out on the end of his sharp knife. She had not seemed very pale, but certainly she had seemed extremely frightened.

And when a snake had slid across their path one afternoon, she had screamed out.

He wondered why he had to add up all of these signs of weakness and join them to her singing, her gay good nature, in order to establish her full character of angel? Was it because he suspected the claw beneath the velvet?

When her bed was made up each night, before he retired to his own distant quarters, she had a sisterly way of kissing him on the brow. No one but she would have thought of that. Even an angel might have been a little more careless and kind about it now and then.

But he had fortified himself with a profound resolution—she was angelic—she could not be anything but the most innocent, guileless, harmless of all creatures.

And this was the last evening. They had come in sight of the town of Los Gatos. Tomorrow he would leave her, and she would ride into the place to find her man. His heart felt sick at the thought.

So as she came over toward him when she had finished the scrubbing of the pans, he asked her: "What sort of a fellow is that one of yours down there in Los Gatos, Sally?"

"The finest in the world," said the girl.

"Yeah, sure," he agreed sourly. "But I mean what does he do for a living?"

"Oh, he just gets a living somehow," she answered cheerfully.

"That generally means anyhow," pointed out big Tom Dallas. "What does he do?"

"Almost anything, Tom," she said. "Sometimes he makes money breaking horses. Sometimes he works with cows. But a lot of the time he just goes around being lucky. Oh, it's wonderful."

"Lucky?" said Dallas. "I'll bet it's wonderful. Lucky at cards, maybe?"

"Yes. How did you guess? He's wonderfully lucky at cards."

"I've heard of that kind of luck," answered Dallas with a dark brow. "Maybe he deals faro now and then?"

"Maybe . . . anyhow, he's very lucky."

He knew, with a profound conviction, that the other fellow was a scoundrel and a snake. If the marriage were postponed for another six months—well, he could use a gun again, and perhaps he would be able to perform with it a work useful to the world in general and to the future of Sally in particular.

"You two going to live on luck when you settle down?" he demanded gruffly.

"Why, yes. Just drift along through the beautiful mountains," said the girl. "Just the way that you and I have been doing, Tom. Haven't you been happy?"

He growled a curt answer. "What about the deserts?" he asked.

"Why, I love the deserts, too," said the girl. "Don't you? They're so different."

"Yeah. They're different, all right," he agreed. He built a cigarette thoughtfully. "You got a mighty interesting future ahead of you, Sally," he declared. "I hope you never get bogged down with that man of yours. When are you going to marry him?"

"As soon as he'll let me," said the girl.

"Ha," grunted Dallas. "As soon as he'll let you? Is he likely to hold off?"

"Well, he's never even told me that he loves me," said Sally Jones.

"Great God," groaned Dallas. "What are you doing, Sally?

Chasing a fool who doesn't want you?"

"He might want me. He's looked at me in a very kind way a lot of times," she decided after a moment of thought.

"But . . . !" shouted Dallas. "Marriage . . . what the . . . I mean. . . ."

"I think I'll have to ask him to marry me," said the girl. "That would be the quickest way, don't you think?"

"My God," said Dallas slowly.

"Are you in pain, Tom?" she asked.

"Damn it, no . . . I mean . . . wait a minute, Sally. *Ask* a man to marry you! You wouldn't do that?"

"Why not?"

She turned, and by the firelight he could see the wide glistening of her eyes and her partly separated lips as she waited for his answer.

He leaned suddenly—he could not help it—and kissed her fairly on the mouth.

Then he sprang to his feet. "My God, Sally," he said. "I'm sorry . . . it just sort of happened. . . ."

"Why are you sorry?" asked Sally Jones. "I liked it, didn't you?"

A shuddering weakness passed through him. "Sally," he said, "you're only a child. You're only a baby. You don't know about life. Now, look here. I'm going to wait out here on the mountain after you go into Los Gatos. I'm going to wait for two or three days. And after you see your man, if everything doesn't go just the way you expect . . . the way you want it to. . . ."

"Tom, you're not going to send me into Los Gatos alone, are you?"

He was stunned. "If you go into the town in full daylight you're perfectly all right, Sally. And . . . you see . . . it would be hard for me to go into that place, really."

"Why would it, Tommy?" she asked. She turned on her side

31

and rested her chin on the palm of her hand and looked up at him.

She was, of course, not only an angel but also a mere child at heart. He would not take advantage of her—the way that skunk in Los Gatos probably would. How did it happen that the man never had told her he loved her?

"Why don't you want to go into Los Gatos?"

"Why, it's a rather long story. But the boss . . . the mayor . . . the *alcalde* . . . the *jefe* . . . the whole gang of them would like to take my innards out and hang them on a pole. I mean, Sally, they don't like me."

"They don't like you?" wondered the girl. "How silly of them."

"They're Mexicans," he explained dubiously.

"But what silly Mexicans. I love you, Tommy. I should think everybody would love you."

"Would you, indeed?" he said dourly. "Well, the short of it is that everybody doesn't. Quite a few don't. But having you like me makes me able to tell the rest of them to go to hell."

"Of course I do. Higher than the sky and deeper than the sea. But why don't the people in Los Gatos like you?"

"Oh, Mexicans are a nervous lot of people, Sally," he told her gravely. "They're not like us. I happened to disturb them a little, a couple of times, and they seem to remember the grudge. Funny."

"I should think so," she agreed. "I never heard of anything so silly. Do you mean that it would be dangerous for you to ride into Los Gatos tomorrow?"

"Well . . . sort of," he said. He thought of the *rurales*, and the colonel of the soldiers at the *presidio*, and the political chief of the whole works. "Sort of dangerous," he repeated.

"What started all the trouble?" she asked.

"Margarita," he remembered aloud, but softly.

"Oh, a girl?" asked Sally brightly.

"Ah . . . why . . . the fact is there's a church of *Santa* Margarita, or something like that. I was tired and sat down on the steps one night. . . ."

"Poor Tommy," she said.

He finished hurriedly: "And then the trouble all started. Afterward, of course, I had to come back there."

"Why did you have to come back?"

"They dared me to . . . I mean, there was business that called me back."

"Margarita?" asked Sally Jones.

He was stunned by the question. It shot electric thrills of fear and of doubt all through him. "Why, no," he said.

She stood up and stretched. He could have stretched out his arm and embraced her. Perhaps she would not mind. Perhaps she would like that, also. But it would only prove that he was contemptible, taking advantage of her. So he stood up, also.

"I won't ask you to take me into town tomorrow morning," she said slowly. "I'll go by myself."

"I'll feel like a dog, Sally."

"How silly, Tommy dear," she said. "Good night."

He leaned for the accustomed procedure. She put her hands against his face and then, instead of kissing his forehead, touched his lips with hers.

"I do love you, Tommy," she said. "There's nobody in the world like you. Not one."

She turned away from him with a bowed head, but it seemed to him, as he looked after her, that her shoulders were quivering, either with suppressed sobs or laughter, and he could not tell which. Nor would he ask.

He went to his blanket, gave himself a roll in it, and lay down to look at the stars.

V

He had not been asleep long. In fact, the stars had hardly seemed to blink and shiver once before he was wide awake again. Perhaps he had slept longer than he thought because the moon had moved a good distance toward the zenith.

Something brought him instantly alert, although he could not tell what it was beyond the whisper of the night wind. . . .

He sat up. At once there was a cutting whisper through the air; a thin film of shadow dropped down before his eyes, and instantly a lariat jerked hard about his chest and elbows. Another shadow at the same time came whistling, and he was caught in another noose, while a loud voice yelled in Spanish: "He is ours! Victory! El Tigre! He is ours! He is ours! Come quickly with guns!"

They came running, a dozen of them, rising from behind the rocks.

"El Tigre!" It was a whole year since he had heard them snarling that pet name for him behind his desperate heels as he fled through the town. Perhaps he had really looked like a tiger to them, as they had seemed so many cats to him.

His first thought was for the girl, and he shouted: "Quick . . . Sally . . . ride! They've got me!"

One of the panting Mexicans stopped in the task of fastening the hands of big Tom Dallas behind his back, and called out: "Do you hear him, *señorita?*"

And, for an answer, there floated into the ears of Dallas the clear, sweet laughter of the girl.

He did not hear it. He could not and would not hear it. It was magic—a transformation of the entire world. This monstrosity could not be.

"Here," said a man in glistening uniform as he rode up on a splendid horse. "Here, friends, let me see him. Aha! El Tigre, we are glad to see you again. We are so delighted that, as you see, we have come a little beyond the gates of the town to welcome you." He began to laugh.

It was, in fact, the commandant, Colonel José Oñate. In addition, he was the father of this Margarita. His hands were on his hips, opening and closing into fists. A tremor of his body made the reflection of the moon tremble also on his bright ornaments.

The other Mexicans jerked Tom Dallas to his feet.

"He's numb with terror," said one of them.

Sally, thought Dallas bitterly, *did I hear you? Did I hear you laugh?*

Yes, and now he heard her again. She came, riding her pinto that danced in the moonlight as though even the mustang enjoyed this fine jest.

"Dear old Tommy," said the girl. "The only safe place in the world for you is Los Gatos. I hated to do it, but it had to be done."

He stared helplessly. His mind would not take the thing in.

"He won't believe," said the colonel. "But, after a while, he will know that he is not dreaming. Oh, there are ways of waking him up."

It *was* like a dream, a frightful nightmare.

They flung him on his horse with his face to the tail of it. They bound his feet beneath its belly. And they carried Tom Dallas in triumph back to the town.

A thing like this capture of El Tigre was not to be taken lightly, so the entry was not made in haste. Swift riders scurried off to warn the town of what was about to take place. And as they approached the old gates with their crumbling stone wall at each side, the armed men formed in deep files on either side of the prisoner, and the colonel himself rode gallantly at the head of the party. He rode with a naked sword in his hand, looking with gloomy valor to his right and to his left, as if at any moment a desperate attack might be made to set the prisoner free.

But there were no such attacks. Young men ran out to make insulting remarks and gestures at El Tigre. And the whole crowd pressed in and shouted its exultation.

One old hag ran like an active spirit beside the horse of Tom Dallas, shouting: "A woman took him! A woman made him prisoner!"

And everyone who heard her yelled with delight again and again.

He had not seen Sally after the moment of his capture, but he had another view of her in the bright moonlight of the crowded plaza. For, higher than most of the others, he was able to make out a huge American standing up in a buckboard, and beside him, perched still higher on the seat of the wagon, was Sally Jones. She was waving her hat from side to side above her head. She was laughing!

The big man laughed, also. He had a beard that made him look more formidable still. And Tom Dallas wondered what his face would be like if, in a few handfuls, that beard were torn away from it.

But only one thing mattered—the girl was gone. She was lost to him. She was not only lost but her whole memory was destroyed. And under Dallas's fifth rib was injected the poisonous knowledge that she had made a fool of him from the very first. What laughter must have been shaking her, really, when she turned from him that very night. What laughter when she had kissed him good night.

And what could he do to her? Nothing. She was a woman; his hands were tied. Well, his hands would be tied still more securely before they led him out to a gallows. Or, perhaps, since he had not actually taken life in the town, he would be merely left to rot for an indefinite number of years in the jail. Such things had happened in Mexico, and such things would happen again.

Yonder was the political *jefe,* the very top man of the town, and he was standing at the top of the broad steps of the jail. It was more than a jail. Once it had been a Spanish castle, and, although some of the upper stories had fallen and been partially cleared away, enough remained to make a jail big enough and strong enough for all of the uses of the men of Los Gatos.

He looked up, hearing, as it were, voices from the sky, and seeing that men and boys were perched on top of the roof, screeching their delight. Truly it was a town of cats, and he, just as truly, was the mouse that they had caught.

The heavy doors of the jail opened. They closed with a mighty bang behind him, shutting out the tumult of the crowd—shutting out life, also, and leaving before him only clammy coldness and the dimness of an altered existence.

Into this fate a girl had drawn him, laughing. If only he had remained back there in Spring Water, to wait for the coming of the gunman, Sam Richmond.

The colonel himself was conducting the examination of the prisoner. The colonel himself was counting over the hundreds of dollars—and the whole wad of money was transferred from the pocket of Dallas to the wallet of the man of war. The empty revolver, also, he took. "As a memento of El Tigre before his claws were clipped," he said, laughing.

"Perhaps there is something more, hidden in his clothes?" suggested the colonel.

In a trice Tom Dallas was stripped almost to the skin. The jailors almost tore the clothes in their eagerness to take the loot.

The colonel, stepping close to Dallas, murmured in English: "I shall tell Margarita that you are here. I shall tell her that you are waiting for her."

They took Tom Dallas down a torturous flight of stone steps

that wound endlessly, and with each descending flight the air began to grow more damp, more cold, and through his almost naked body struck a penetrating chill. At last, in the bottom of the dungeon, a heavy door—barred across with iron and rodded up and down with heavy strips of the same metal—was opened. He had a glimpse of the interior—a set of irons against the wall, and a matted quantity of moldy straw, straw so damp and rotten that it had turned black in spots.

He was not thrown into the cell at once. First, one of the guards said to him: "Do you remember me, *señor?*"

He looked sharply, drawn by the unexpected courtesy of this voice, and he saw before him a tall man in the uniform of a captain. His face was terribly scarred on the right side, the scar tissue drawing violently on the rest of the flesh, so that he had an invincible squint.

"I am that same Mateo Bardi," he said. "Do you remember, *señor?*"

He smiled, as he spoke, and the scar seemed to wrench the smile apart and transform his entire face into an epic ugliness. The naked devil looked out from his eyes.

Tom Dallas could remember. It was the worthy captain who had baited the trap for him on the first occasion by sending him the forged letter that pretended to come from the girl. It was Captain Mateo Bardi who had been on the spot, also, to supervise the capture of the *gringo,* and it had been over the body of the same captain that he had made the first stride of his escape.

Tom Dallas's bullet had struck the captain above the cheek bone and had ranged down through the chin.

"My life is now ruined," said the captain, continuing the horror of that smile. "Let me see what I can do to ruin yours, *señor.* Day and night I shall remain near to see that you are kept safely and comfortably." Then he ordered his men to throw Tom Dallas into the cell.

They did exactly that. Half a dozen powerful hands grabbed Dallas and hurled him into the cell. His head struck against the wall, and, as his senses gradually returned, he found Captain Mateo Bardi locking his legs into the heavy, rusted irons that were fastened by a chain into a mighty staple sunk into the solid stone masonry at the foot of the wall.

"So, *señor*, compose yourself for many peaceful days," said the captain, and withdrew.

The door slammed, shutting out the last ray of light, and the heavy bolt ground home.

Tom Dallas, in the rôle of El Tigre, sat down, cross-legged, on the rotten straw and turned in his mind certain thoughts, as a cook might turn grilling fowl on a spit. Being what he was, he was not weakened by disaster. Rather, it added to him a certain strange, incalculable force.

The big American of the beard and Sally Jones—his mind rested chiefly on them, and on the last picture of their laughter. He could not touch the girl except through the man, but what a touch that would be, if ever his hand could fall on the fellow who had such good luck at cards. Colonel Oñate, also, deserved a call. And perhaps in the entire town of Los Gatos, only Margarita was not laughing. Or, perhaps, she was. If Sally Jones could be what she was, even the dark, passionate eyes of Margarita might be as fickle as quicksilver.

He regretted with a sick heart that he had forbidden himself to carry a loaded gun for a year. If he had had one—no, the girl's treachery had been too complete and the ropes had fallen about his arms before he could have used a revolver. But she had told them in the first place that he was unarmed or perhaps they never would have dared to come so close to him. That was the vital spot in the explanation.

The ankle irons were too small for his big bones and they

began to hurt him. He put down his hand and touched them. In a blind frenzy of protest, he caught at the chain and jerked violently.

The chain rattled loudly and startled him with the noise that he was making. But it seemed to him that it had yielded a little to his pull. That was folly, for iron chains might be snapped but they cannot give.

Seriously, steadily with all his might, he pulled on the chain again, and this time he was sure that something gave—not the chain, of course, but perhaps the staple sunk into the stone.

The hope struck him like a fist between the eyes. Such an exultation burst upward in him that he had to grind his teeth to keep from shouting. He tried the chain, this way and that, up and down.

And by degrees the big iron staple was issuing from the wall. He worked at it patiently now, and a final pull brought the thing clear—a full foot of rusted iron pin, rough toward the end so that it almost made a point. On the side there was another rough spot to show where the original bend had been of the angle iron that locked the bar in place in the stone.

Already he felt the wildness in his blood, telling him that he was free. And yet he knew that he had taken not so much as the first real step toward liberty.

The locked door, the winding flights of steps, the guard established by the worthy Captain Bardi nearby, and the other guards above—all of these had to be passed. But the first step is the most important, and his raging hope doubled his strength.

He could walk with fairly comfortable steps, holding up the length of chain and the bolt in his hands. The free bolt was now not a means of holding him but a tool through which he could work further toward his freedom. The lock of the door he could not manage, of course. It was an old-fashioned bolt, merely thrust into a ponderous socket in the wall and engaging, with a lifting handle, in an iron slot fastened to the door. A child could open it without a key from the outside, but from the inside it was as impregnable as the most mysterious labor of the locksmith.

The iron slabs that covered the door were too strong, also. But there remained the wood over which they were laid. The first stroke of the sharp bolt point against the inner wooden surface was a triumph, for it crunched deeply into the plank. Time that had rusted iron in this subterranean vault had rotted the wood, also.

He fumbled to the side, found the edge of the door, and guessed with care at the height and the size of the lock. Above this calculated point he began to dig into the decayed wood with the point of the bolt. It ate rapidly in. He had to use some care, now, for fear his noise might be heard in the outer corridor. In another moment, he had worked the point of the bolt through and it was grinding against one of the iron bindings of the door. He worked to the side of this. With every moment of labor the wood seemed to grow softer for his tool. At last he punched the point straight through into empty air.

Once started, that hole was soon enlarged. He could push three fingers through. He could pass his entire hand through the gap. And, looking through, he saw a thin streak of light like an eye that waited and watched for him.

Reaching through, his hand found the bolt handle, lifted it, worked it gradually back to avoid making the old iron creak in its socket. The door, softly pressed, gradually swung open before him. And he stood now in the lowest corridor of the old dungeon.

He leaned against the wall, to draw breath and to plan. And as he leaned his shoulders against the wall, he could think of nothing except to go straight forward.

The noise of the chain was the chief thing to be guarded

against. He stripped off his underwear and wrapped it as well as he could around the rusted iron.

The glint of light that he had seen appeared now as a roughly etched line of gleaming yellow that outlined the next door in the hallway. When he put his ear close to this, he felt, rather than heard, the vibration of voices. Immediately afterward, he made out the clear, cutting voice of the captain. Pressing his ear close to the crack, he could make out the words.

". . . and first there is sorrow that makes weeping, and then the cold, quiet sorrow that is despair. Then some men go mad, and other men fall into a stupor. The madmen die, and the stupid ones may live thirty years, beyond pain because they no longer have the nerves with which to feel it."

"The *gringo?*" asked the captain.

"What will he be like?"

"He will go mad," answered the rough voice. "The people call him El Tigre, don't they? Well, he'll never stop snarling. I saw a wolf once that smashed all its teeth chewing at the chain that held it. Free men cannot put up with imprisonment very well, but wild men like El Tigre go mad."

"Good, Pedro," chuckled the captain. "Take another drink. I wish his brain would rot a grain a day, and, when he's raving, I would let the *Señorita* Margarita put her eyes on him . . . when his body's starved, and dirty, and his brain is gone, eh?"

The other laughed. "I can see the reason why you hate him, Captain."

The captain, in a sudden rage at this impertinence, shouted: "Get out of my sight, you fool! Go up and send down Juan. I'll remember you for this."

There was a desperate attempt at an apology, the sound of a smacking blow, and then the muttering of the captain as he walked up and down, wrapped in his affronted pride.

Here Tom Dallas tried the bolt of the door gingerly. It gave at once. He had not much time. The second guard would return immediately. And the best device that occurred to Dallas was simply to let the door sag slowly open. A gust of air struck it and pushed it wide with a sudden groaning sound.

The captain called on a saint or two in a burst of terror. But since nothing appeared at the door, he presently muttered that the infernal old castle was rotting to pieces and all the locks giving way.

Having said this, he approached the door cautiously and stuck his head out into the darkness. It made a perfect target. Tom Dallas could not have missed if he tried. And he exploded the fullness of his weight and strength with a driving blow that thudded heavily against the side of the captain's head.

Afterward he caught the falling body in his arms.

VI

The keys came first. They were easily found because there were a full thirty of them on the ring, but at least twenty-five of the thirty had to be tried before the right one slipped into the locks of the leg irons and set Tom Dallas free. By that time, the captain was stirring and groaning faintly.

He was a big man, so that when Dallas ripped off the trousers and jacket of the captain, he was able to step into them. The shoes would not do, and Dallas had to be content with his stocking feet.

Captain Bardi stared, fascinated, at the *gringo,* and then down at his own half-naked body.

"Walk before me, Bardi," said Dallas. "I could make you silent forever and save myself a good deal of time . . . but I have a reason for saving you."

The captain shrugged. "Do as you please with me, but you will never escape from the prison, *señor.* There are twenty men in the guardroom above the stairs, and there is no way out except through that room."

"Bardi," said Dallas, "I've taken two steps on the way to freedom and now I'll make it at a jump."

"El Tigre," murmured Bardi, and said no more.

He walked obediently before Dallas down the dark of the corridor. At the first door at which he arrived, Dallas turned the heavy bolt, pulled the door open, and exposed, by the dim lantern light that streamed after them, a bearded giant ironed to the walls, a man more than half naked, with a beard like Spanish moss dripping from his face.

"Do you know Captain Bardi?" asked Dallas.

"I know that son-of-a-dog," growled the rusty voice of the big prisoner.

"He's come to keep you company," said Dallas, and thrust the gallant captain straight before him into the cell.

He saw the great hands of the captive rise to greet Bardi. And he closed the door in haste over the frantic screech of the captain.

Then he returned to the small room in which Bardi had been sitting on guard. Already footsteps were descending. He could hear a Mexican saying: "You can see him, *Señor* Richmond, but you cannot have him. We of Los Gatos have a certain need to keep him here. When he grows long hair and a beard, he will be good to show in the plaza during fiestas. It will discourage crime and make our people proud of Colonel Oñate, who captured him."

The Colt of Captain Bardi, carefully emptied of cartridges, was now in the hand of Dallas. He waited, half crouched, at the side of the door that opened on the stairs.

Sam Richmond had come, then, even as quickly as this. Perhaps it was part of the girl's plan to warn Richmond and have him on the spot when Dallas was snared. What devil had inspired her? What evil had he ever done to her?

He heard Richmond saying: "That man murdered my brother, and, by God, I'll have him for myself one way or another."

The door was pushed open. Dallas, standing halfway across the room, was running straight at it in the silence of his stockinged feet the first instant it stirred, and, as it opened wide, he broke like a thunderbolt right upon the two men.

He had of Richmond only a vague impression of bigness and fine proportions before the barrel of his gun rang like a bell clapper along Sam's head. He heard behind him a frantic yell of: "¡El Tigre! ¡El Tigre! He is loose! Beware!"

He was already up at the head of the stairs as a door was opened in his face and a dozen soldiers crowded out.

"What is it?" one of them shouted to him, seeing him dimly in the half light.

"Below, there . . . El Tigre. . . . I go to have the outer doors closed. . . ."

Half a dozen of the men poured down the steps. Then the voice of the soldier who had guided Richmond down was heard screeching: "There! He is there! Catch El Tigre, in the name of God!"

There was nothing for it but to plunge straight out into the brilliantly lighted guardroom, filled with armed men as it was. He ran as a snipe flies, dodging. The door was of no use. He could not get through there, where two men with bayoneted rifles, stood at ready. The window was open, but four armed men were rising from the bench that stood in front of it. Nevertheless, the window was the only possible chance. The empty revolver he leveled before him and charged with a word-less roar tearing from his throat.

Three of the soldiers dived to either side to get away from him. The fourth man caught up his carbine and fired straight at the breast of Dallas. A side-step made that bullet miss, and a clip from the heavy Colt barrel sent the soldier reeling. Dallas bounded, like the beast he was named for, through the deep casement.

What he saw in the moonlight was bad enough—a roof almost twenty feet below him, and below the roof, on either side, the streets still crowded. A drainpipe of rusty iron ran down past the window. He swung out onto this, handed himself down two arm lengths, and dropped as the window above him filled with guns and faces as the soldiers yelled: "¡El Tigre! You below! He is loose! Beware! ¡El Tigre! Capture the devil!"

There was more shouting, but it was drowned by the rapid explosions of rifles as Dallas fell on the tiles of the roof and rolled rapidly down the slope. By spreading his legs apart, he was able to check the spinning of his body, but he could get no handhold on the rapidly sloping tiles. Not till his body had shot into the thinness of space did his hands grip the gutter at the edge of the roof.

It sagged, ripping away with an almost human screech. And Dallas whirled in the air as he dropped.

The cluster of people below him had no time to scatter. He aimed his feet at the breast of one and knocked the man headlong. That broke the fall. He dropped, rolling in the dust of the street, and came to his feet, sprinting.

It was like falling into a hornet's nest. A knife reached for him and sliced through the jacket that flared out behind his back. Bullets hummed past his head. Every one of the Mexicans in that street seemed armed, all were fleet of foot, and the whole body of them rushed for him.

Ahead, behind him, the shout was always: "¡El Tigre! ¡El Tigre!"

To the left a narrow lane opened between two adobes, where a peddler had posted his cart, heaped high with goods.

Dallas made for it. He jumped high, struck the top of the

load in spite of his efforts, and rolled in the lane beyond in a vast clattering of pots, pans, and trinkets.

But he was up. There had to be lightning in his feet and steel in his body tonight if ever. If only a loaded gun were in his hand, he could blast his way through this—but there was only the pretense of the empty six-shooter.

Down the lane he fled, turned sharply to the right into the next street, saw it alive with people, and dodged right again through the door of a house, past the owner, who sat stunned in the threshold.

Once inside the hut, Dallas knew that he was trapped. There was no window, no rear door. The place was a solid box for which the chimney and the door gave the only ventilation.

He turned, despairing, and saw the little man at the door standing with a pointing arm. It was easy to see, now, why the man had not come to his feet sooner. He was a cripple with a wooden leg below the right knee. But he was shouting: "That way . . . around the corner, between my house and Pedro Gil's!"

The thronging, the shouting instantly began to pour past the doorway, then the uproar of the pursuit ranged farther away. Now and again there was an outbreak of gunfire, but the instant of danger had blown over for big Tom Dallas. He rested his weight on one knee, panting heavily.

And the householder turned at last from the door. "Your gun . . . why did you not use it, *Señor* El Tigre?" asked the cripple.

"It's empty. I have a vow not to carry a loaded gun through this year," panted Dallas. The Mexican would understand a vow. "Why were you kind to me?" asked Dallas. "You are in danger, friend, if the *jefe* or the colonel find out that you have given me a hiding place. Was some American once kind to you?"

"Very kind!" snarled the little man. "The *americanos* were so kind that they took a burden away from me. They took away the weight of half a leg. That was their kindness, *señor*. Two bullets through the knee. Why? Because I was a damned greaser, and they were noble *americanos*."

Dallas listened, amazed at all this. Next he heard his host say: "But when I was young, I was a hunter, and I love the sport. A thousand against one is not fair. Even a rabbit is given a running start. But you, El Tigre, break out of the bottom of the prison and fly through the air . . . how have you come here?"

In brief words, Dallas told him.

The cripple laughed a little. "They will catch you. You will never get out of the town. The walls will be ringed with armed men, waiting for you. Searching parties will go through every house in the town. They will catch you . . . and because of what the *gringos* have done to me, I am glad that you will be caught. However, they will never take a man like you alive. Let it be a great run and a noble ending. *Señor* El Tigre, I am a richer man because you have entered my house. You shall dine with me. I have half a bottle of red wine . . . a little old and flat and sour . . . but wine, nevertheless, that I was keeping for the next fiesta. I have also tortillas, such as a man can make with his own clumsy hands, and some good *frijoles*. You must eat with me, and talk a little. God, God . . . I am hungrier for a man's talk than any famished man for food."

VII

From that man, Pedrillo, Dallas learned much that he wanted to know. That big American who wore the beard was, in fact, one John Leffler, who had a big house in town—a house with a garden around it, a beautiful thing to see. Also, he had a mine back in the hills. He was not very young. He was said to be a just man. And like all Americans he was terribly rich.

That did not seem to fit with the description that the girl had given of her lover, he who would not say that he loved her. If

Leffler were the man, perhaps he knew her much too well to become sentimental. Perhaps he could tell certain stories about her past that would be worth hearing, and that was why he was in no haste to marry the seductive, lying wildcat with her gentle ways, her blue eyes, her devilish brain.

Of the fine jacket and trousers of the captain, a gift was made to this Pedrillo, who hated all Americans but loved a brave man. Pedrillo, in exchange, gave to Dallas some stain of the black walnut that turned the face and the body of Dallas almost black. He gave him, also, a cheap cotton shirt, a pair of cotton trousers, and some *huaraches,* or sandals, for his feet. He even gave him a great straw hat with a crown shaped like a funnel and a vast, ragged brim. This was the guise in which Dallas stood at the door.

"I shall remember you, Pedrillo," he said.

"Only in heaven, El Tigre, or in the hell where you will surely go with the rest of the *gringos.* But if you have wings and a miracle and manage to fly away, forget me, friend, but do one kind thing for some Mexican, in your own land."

He grasped the hand of Dallas, and the big man stepped instantly into the street.

Soldiers from the fort went jingling in squads here and there in the streets, and a long file of infantry went by. It was plain that Pedrillo was right and that the town of Los Gatos was devoting itself with a single mind toward the recapture of El Tigre. El Tigre himself, smoking a cigarette and feeling the dust of the street sift over his dark-stained toes, chuckled a little. He was, he knew, in the very middle of a trap, but he was of a nature that could not worry until a gun was clapped to his head.

He went toward the house and garden of Leffler and presently saw the loom of the trees, and the high wall that contained them. He saw more than this—the gilded coach of Colonel

49

Oñate himself standing at the gate. As military commandant of the town he used the most splendid article of the old ceremonial days—a very bright, carved coach so heavy that it was generally drawn by from four to six horses. There were four fine white horses with plumes nodding above their headstalls in front of the coach, this night. A coachman sat on the box; a footman stood at the head of the horses.

And the American, sauntering on the other side of the street, said—*"Bah!"*—very audibly. For of what real use was a coach like this, so heavy that it would soon be broken up if it ventured far along the rocky roads and trails that led out of the town of Los Gatos?

Dallas crossed the street, made sure that no one was watching, and was instantly up on the top of the wall. There he lay flat and took heed of his surroundings. Across the street, along the roofs, he saw half a dozen furtive figures creeping, and the moonlight glimmered on their weapons. They were hunting for the fugitive. By this time there would be a fine price on the head of El Tigre—truly this was a city of the cats.

Inside the garden, he could see the great trunks of the trees and the glistening hedges of shrubbery, and behind these the lighted windows of the house itself, most of them shuttered so that only stray gleams escaped into the night.

Approaching through the brush, he almost touched what seemed a tall, narrow shrub.

The shrub said: "Felipe?"

"Yes," answered Dallas.

"You look six inches taller."

"I'm at least as tall as you think," said Dallas.

The other chuckled. "The night makes everything bigger," he said. "Rub your eyes open. We may see something."

"Do you think El Tigre would be fool enough to try to come here?"

"He is not a fool. He *is* a tiger, and he's hungry enough to eat up trouble. Did you hear what happened at the *juzgado?*"

"I heard some lies," said Dallas.

He went on. He was through the circle of *guardias* that had been thrown around the house and he could move more freely, now.

It was not hard to find the place where the crowd had gathered. The drowsy humming of voices poured out from one source, and now and again hearty laughter peeled. Moreover, two big windows were wide open to the cool of the night. He climbed up on the ledge of the foundation and looked through into a big dining hall where the long table was ringed with many men, and one woman.

The woman was Sally Jones.

Among the men he spotted the fat face and profligate belly of the political *jefe* of the town; the splendid uniform of the colonel was at this moment making an entrance through the doorway, and yonder was Leffler, the big man of the beard, rising to greet the man of war.

The colonel was badly shaken. He came in, wagging his head. With a raised hand he put aside all comfort.

"Men are not what they used to be," he declared. He took a glass of brandy, and swallowed it.

"Just what happened at the jail?" asked the sweet voice of Sally Jones.

"What? Treason and deviltry," said the colonel. "The man has, as you know, the strength of a fiend. With his hands he burst the iron staple out of the wall. . . ."

"Nonsense!" exclaimed a voice in very bad Spanish. And following the sound, the eyes of Dallas came to the face of Sam Richmond. Seen by a full light, he looked even more formidable than he had appeared in the gloom of the stairway back there at the jail. And now dimly Dallas could remember having seen this

51

prominent forehead, the slightly concave but handsome face, and the neat mustaches.

Far away in events, not long ago in time, he recalled guns booming in a narrow ravine, a wild bellowing and trampling of cattle clashing their horns, and a determined rush of the cattle rustlers to clear the pass that was blocked by big Tom Dallas and one poor rancher.

Why was Dallas on the side of the law that day? Simply because he was always on the side of the underdog to challenge the main chance. Very gallantly the rustlers had pressed home their charge, led by this same Sam Richmond, until a bullet from the gun of Dallas had dropped him across the neck of his horse. The rest of the rustlers had fled, at that, and the wildly racing horse had carried the wounded man away after them.

That was where he had first seen Sam Richmond. Perhaps the report of that fight had been what brought Jerry Richmond stalking out onto the porch of the mountain trail-side saloon to murder the man who had planted lead in the body of his brother.

The whole mystery began to clear up a little.

"*You* may say what you please," said the colonel sternly, "but I tell you nothing except the actual facts. This man or devil, El Tigre, ripped the staple out of the wall. We have it now at the jail and can show the place where the strong iron was fractured at the angle. A horse could not have done the thing, but El Tigre did it. We have the proof. And then he smashed his hand through the wood of the door. . . ."

A general exclamation followed this remark. He went on, and finished with: "And he laid poor Captain Bardi senseless with a blow, stripped off his clothes, donned them, and, to keep Bardi from giving the alarm, flung him into a cell."

There was a general murmur of stupefaction from the crowd. But the girl said in her clear, bell-like voice: "He could have silenced Bardi in a shorter way, couldn't he?"

That comment was delicious music to big Tom Dallas.

But the colonel replied, laughing gruffly: "Ah, you think it was a mercy? In fact he threw poor Bardi into a cell where a crazy giant has been sitting for ten years, and by the time we heard the screams of Bardi, he had been almost killed by the giant. That is the sort of a man this El Tigre is. Frantic and terrible . . . not to be believed. Think how he dashed you and the sergeant aside to get up the stairs, *Señor* Richmond."

The girl turned sharply and stared at Sam Richmond, who turned a deep crimson. The servants, who were moving, soft-footed, around the table to serve the guests at that midnight confection, paused and stared at Richmond, also.

"And then," went on the excited colonel, "he plunged through the guardroom, knocks twenty guards to this side and that, ducks a bullet fired in his face . . . the guard swore that he must have turned the lead aside with his breath . . . and leaps through a window to the roof twenty feet below. . . ."

"Hurray!" shouted Sally Jones. And she began to laugh and clap her hands together.

The bearded Leffler broke in: "Excuse her, Colonel. She is like a child . . . she loves to hear stories about wild men."

"Well, God protect her if she ever should fall into the hands of *that* wild man," said the colonel. "What a lucky thing that, as she was riding through the hills, she happened to see the monster making his camp and was able to bring us to the spot. What a lucky thing was that, my friends."

"Why lucky?" asked the *jefe*. "He is gone again, eh?"

"Gone from the jail but not from the town," said the colonel. "We have him. No . . . it is better this way, because now we shall enjoy the hunt. My men are posted on every inch of the walls. Do you see? There is not a human soul who can leave the town of Los Gatos except myself."

"Ha?" said the *jefe*. "Not even I?"

"Not during this emergency," said the colonel.

"And I tell you all," said Sam Richmond, "even while I know that it must sound like boasting, that I would like nothing so much as to meet this fellow . . . this El Tigre, as you call him . . . this same Tom Dallas . . . alone. Man to man." He leaned a little forward in his chair, smiling faintly, a smile that made his short mustaches bristle, and suddenly Tom Dallas was aware that this was the king of the cats in Los Gatos.

A polite silence followed this statement from Richmond, and then the girl turned and touched the man's arm.

"After all this, do you still think so, Sam?" she asked.

"What have I come all this distance for except the chance?" he demanded angrily.

"Well," said the girl, "when I heard a year ago, how one man had ripped right through an entire town, I wouldn't believe my ears, but now I'm beginning to believe."

There was an enthusiastic murmur of agreement from the Mexicans.

And a new poison was injected into Dallas. She had known from the first. She had selected Los Gatos for her mysterious journey simply because she wanted to land him in a trap. Listen to her now.

"When you wrote to me, Uncle John, it sounded like a fairy tale."

Uncle John? Was Leffler her uncle? Certainly it was not Leffler who was her lover. It was another man—about the size of Tom Dallas. One who drifted through the world even as Dallas drifted; one who bucked any game of chance, again like Dallas, and who else was there present who filled all of these elements of description? Why, there was Sam Richmond, of course. He was the man.

The colonel was saying: "I have brought you the gun of El Tigre, *señorita*. Without you, we never should have had our hands on the villain, we never might have had him trapped here in Los Gatos. Take this revolver to remind you of what you have done."

And he presented the weapon to Sally Jones, while she accepted it with a bow. How full of grace she was—and how full of hell!

"I'm going to put it away now, in my room," she said. "Besides, it's time for me to leave the gentlemen to their plans for capturing El Tigre. I drink to your fortune."

She lifted the glass with a smile and a laugh. It was rather odd that she did not attempt to taste the contents.

VIII

Like the tiger after which they called him, slinking and soft-footed, Dallas left the window, reached a side balcony, and was instantly swarming up the pillar that supported it. It seemed to him that he could die contented if he could penetrate the motive of the girl in leading him into captivity. It was a trick worthy of any clever scout, but it was a trick that only a woman could have played, using her beauty, her pretended frankness, and childish innocence to make a fool of him.

What had her real past been like?

There were lighted windows, above, and one of them was undoubtedly her room. One window stood wide open, the lace curtains fanning idly in and out through the gap, and with a cursory glance he saw the room was empty. But his survey had been far too quick. He was gliding by the window when he discovered, right behind the flap of the lace curtains, a brown-faced house servant who had remained unseen—doubtless because of the white clothes he wore, which matched closely the curtains themselves.

The fellow had the stricken, gaping look of one who sees a ghost, and the grasp of Dallas was instantly on his windpipe.

As Dallas strode in through the window, the poor man dropped to his knees, whispering: "Kindness of God . . . have mercy, El Tigre. I have never lifted a hand. . . ."

Terror left the poor devil little better than a pulp. A ragged fragment of the curtain formed a gag, and Dallas left the *mozo* tied, hand and foot, in a corner of the room but only after he had asked: "The room of the new *señorita,* where is it?"

When he had the answer to that, he was equipped for the next step in his adventure. It would be the most dangerous of all, perhaps. If she had had brains enough to make a fool of him before, she might have brains enough to do it again.

He passed out into the big upper hall, where a carpet silenced his footfalls, and passed two doors and on to the one that the *mozo* had named as that of the girl. Inside, he could hear her singing softly—one of those very songs that he had heard so often on the trail to Los Gatos. Then, slowly, soundlessly he turned the handle of the door and pushed it gradually open wide enough for him to step inside.

She was turned half away from him, reclining on a couch and holding in her hands the old, empty Colt that had been his friend through so many years of life.

She was so intent on her work that he was able to cross the room and stand quietly beside her before she looked up with a sudden jerk of the head. The color ran out of her face.

He was cruelly glad to see that. And yet it hurt him, also.

Then she stood up. "Well," she said, "this is clever, too, Tommy. I suppose about the last place they'll look for you will be in this house."

He was amazed at the quiet calmness of her voice. Her color, also, was returning at once, and not in a guilty flush.

"By the Lord, Sally," he said, "I don't think you're afraid of me, even."

"Afraid of you? Afraid of what you think, but not of what

you'll do," she answered. And then that crooked smile flashed at him. Like the smile that he had loved, her soul was twisted, also, he told himself.

"Still, there's a lot of danger in a fellow who'll kiss a poor little helpless girl when she's all alone in the mountains," said Sally.

"It's a joke, all right," said Dallas. He nodded at her. "The queer part was that I was in love with your crooked self, Sally."

"Were you?" she asked.

"You knew that, I suppose?"

"I guessed it."

"The straight of your face," he said. "That's what beats me. I can't get over the way you kept your face all the while, Sally."

She looked at him and answered slowly: "I didn't. Sometimes I had to sing, all at once. You may have noticed that I was laughing a good deal when singing."

"Yeah, I noticed that," he agreed grimly. "I used to think it was just the joy of living and the love of the music that made you laugh when you sang. It was nothing but laughter at me, eh?"

"Just partly," she said.

"And what else?"

"That's not in the book."

"Still have to keep a little mystery?"

"A whole lot, Tommy. There was a time when I thought you'd get to the bottom of my mystery, but now I'm afraid that you never will."

"Afraid?" he said.

"That's what I mean."

"D'you know, Sally, that, if you were a man, I'd take you by the throat and strangle you?" he asked gently.

She ran the tips of her fingers over the soft of her throat. "Yes, you would," she said, nodding. "But a girl is safe in the big chivalrous West, Tommy."

"Yes," he agreed. "You're . . . safe."

"Do you want to curse me?"

"No, not even that. I'd have to find a new brand of words to fit you."

"Try it. I won't mind."

"I'll take that gun and leave you a newer one," he said.

She gave him the old Colt and he put it away under his armpit, in the spring holster. "Captain Bardi used to be proud of having this one," he added, and passed the weapon to her.

She said, looking down at it: "You've never had a loaded gun since you left Spring Water. Why?"

"That's my mystery," he answered sourly.

"But when you left that town, did you know that you wouldn't load a gun all the way to Los Gatos?"

"Yes, I knew that."

All at once she was shuddering as she stared up at him. "Tommy, isn't there any fear in you?" she asked. "Are you all steel and devil? Just the way the Mexicans here say?"

"I don't matter in this deal . . . ," he began.

"To ride clear down here . . . where you knew that you had ten thousand enemies . . . and without a weapon? And then I noticed that you did *not* shoot with Bardi's gun."

"Never mind that," he answered. "I want you to answer me a question. Will you?"

"I hope I can."

"You can, and you're the only person in the world who can. When you came there to Spring Water, that night of the Fourth, were you looking for me?"

"Yes," she said.

"And did you spot me right away at my table?"

"Yes."

"But you waited for me to follow you?"

"I hoped that you'd notice a pretty girl, Tommy."

"You're aware that you're pretty, Sally?" And he was surprised to see her flush.

"I've had to know that," she answered.

"But, Sally, why did you come to Spring Water looking for me? That's what I want to know."

Her lips parted. Then she shook her bead. "It's no good. I can't tell you," she said.

She looked up at him in a hopeless way, so that suddenly he found himself forgetting all that he knew about her and actually swayed forward on the verge of taking her in his arms.

"Damn!" he said through his teeth, rallying himself.

"Ah, Tommy," she said, "are you still a little fond of the old girl, in spite of what she's done?"

And at this moment her smile and the blue of her eyes and the slight, exquisite fragrance that he found in the air, as though left there by her breathing, brought a groan from Dallas's big throat.

"I hoped that I could hate you," he said. "But I don't."

"I'm sorry," said the girl.

"All your life men have loved you, haven't they?"

"Pretty much all my life," she said.

"And how many of them have you loved?" he answered.

"Two," she answered instantly.

"Only two, eh?" Dallas sneered. "One of 'em is the man who you expected to meet in Los Gatos?"

"Yes."

"Richmond, eh?"

"I can't talk in names," she replied.

"I'll tell you something, my dear," he said. "I met this Sam Richmond a long time ago when he was rustling some cows. Mind you, I'm no better than he is, but I don't rustle cows from the little ranchers. We had a run-in where he played second

59

fiddle. Now mind you this, beautiful . . . I'm going to meet the man you love . . . your Sam Richmond . . . again. Write this down in red. I'm going to kill him as sure as hell. . . ."

"Are you?" said the girl.

She seemed to have only the vaguest interest in what he was saying. Her attention was focused on something at the back of his brain.

"I am," he assured her.

"You can't put your hands on a woman, but you're going to kill the man you think she loves?" she went on.

"He needs killing . . . he's a snake," said Dallas.

"That's what a lot of people think."

"By God," murmured Dallas, "I don't think there's a human being in the world you care about. . . ."

"There's one," she said.

"Who is that?"

"You wouldn't believe me," she answered. Then, lifting her hand suddenly, she whispered: "Hush."

He could hear it, then, quite clearly—a far-off multiple creaking sound, very soft, together with a still lighter whispering. He knew suddenly what it meant—the treading of many feet on the carpet of the stairs and of the hall.

IX

Dallas gave the girl one look; she stood straight, expressionless—and then he dived through the window onto the balcony. Almost instantly then, there was a loud shout. A gun cracked in rapid fire from the ground below him. The bullets ripped through the woodwork of the balcony as though through cardboard. Several of the small splinters stung his face. He jerked open a window and jumped through it into darkness at the same time that the head of the pursuit poured from the room of the girl onto the balcony behind him. Their yells resounded as they saw him double into the house.

Fumbling through the dark of the room, he found the doorknob, jerked it open, and stepped straight into a swirling mob that filled the hall.

But he could not turn back because retreat would be blocked. It was only three steps to cross the hall into the next room, and he made those steps with the uniformed figures rushing down the hall toward him, and the few who were close at hand shrank back suddenly, as though from the devil. They would have recovered their nerve for battle in another half second. It was the sudden appearance of the quarry that had made them numb. Long before that half second was ended, he had snatched open a door across the hall and slammed it hard behind him. A twist of the key gave him a moment or two.

There was a small lamp that gave light to the bedchamber. It showed him, beyond the polished glass of the window in which a reflection of the lamp swam, what seemed at first the gesture of a dark, warning arm, but he understood it at once—the limb of one of the great trees that stood near the house.

They were beating on the door behind him; they were rushing it with their shoulders, and, as soon as they made a concerted effort, it would go down.

He jerked the window up. Before him wavered the branches of the tree hardly a yard away. If he caught it, it would let him down like a limber rope, of course, and snap at once. But there was a better chance still.

Climbing out through the window, he stood up on the sill. The moment he was erect his weight toppled him forward. There was nothing for it except to jump but he had already glimpsed a target, and, springing out with all his might, he clutched at a fork of a branch that was well in, just below the level of his head. His hand caught, held.

He heard the door of the room crash down as he climbed

swiftly to a lower branch and crouched there like a vast ape, listening, the tree trunk securely between him and the house.

Below him ran the driveway and in it stood the glimmer of the colonel's coach with the four white horses shining faintly in front of the great carriage. He could see the groom at the heads of the front span. He could see the big coachman running up toward the rear of the coach.

Through the open window above him he heard a voice shouting: "I heard him pull the window open . . . this way he must have gone!"

"He hasn't had time to climb down to the ground," another said. "There's nothing that even an ape could hold on for climbing."

"The other rooms. He went this way!"

The storm of the search spread this way and that, and big Tom Dallas sat on his branch, gathering breath.

Other conversation followed from the window above—the colonel, Leffler, and the girl.

The colonel was in a terrible heat. "Somewhere in the house!" he insisted. "He's somewhere in the house. Even El Tigre isn't a damn' bird!"

"Now, just suppose," said Leffler, "that he dived out of the window into that tree. . . ."

"Would you like to try that?" demanded the colonel.

"I half wish the nervy devil would get away," said Leffler. "What a man . . . what a man."

"You Americans, you are always cool . . . and nothing matters. But my honor and the honor of Los Gatos. Mother of heaven, suppose that he gets through our hands for a third time. All of Mexico will yell with laughter. I shall be disgraced and demoted. I shall be sent to command a horrible little post in the middle of the desert and drink only *pulque* and alkali water. Think of *me, Señor* Leffler, with my jail burst open, my captain half killed, my men flouted, the whole town fooled and laughed at. Think . . . think!"

"I'm thinking," said Leffler. "Those fellows of yours make too much noise, though."

"What happened in your room, my dear?" asked Leffler.

The voice of the girl answered: "I was sitting there, Uncle John, when the door burst open and that giant leaped in . . . he seemed like a giant, and he snatched the gun . . . his own gun . . . out of my hands. I was holding it, and then I was so staggered with terror that I could only stand there. I was . . . staggered, sick, faint. . . ."

"It doesn't sound like you," said her uncle. "I wouldn't think that a whole cage filled with rattlesnakes would blunt your taste for excitement a great deal. You're not laughing at me a little, eh? What about this, Sally?"

"Laughing? At El Tigre?" she said.

"No, no," said the colonel. "No, *Señor* Leffler . . . the poor child . . . how she can even be standing after such a dreadful experience?"

"The whole business of your trip down here . . . it's too infernally mysterious, Sally," said John Leffler. "And suddenly discovering the great El Tigre just before he gets to the town. Something about that hardly washes, Sally. I'm going to ask you some questions, later on."

"Later if you will," said the colonel. "But tonight she must leave your house. She must come to my wife's quarters in the fort. With that devil ranging the town . . . look . . . he has a reason to hold a grudge against your niece. She must be protected. . . ."

"I don't know," said Leffler. "But I suppose that I ought to play safe. I wish you would take her. And give a place to that young man, that Samuel Richmond who wants to meet El Tigre face to face. . . ."

"He would run like a coyote before a wolf," vowed the colonel.

"No," said Leffler, "I've an idea that he means what he says. Take him along. He looks to me like a fellow who would be useful in a pinch."

"I shall take him, then. There is the coach. Wait . . . I shall give orders."

He called more loudly: "Hernando!"

"¿Señor?" called the big coachman.

"Send in Porfilo . . . I have orders. . . ."

X

It was the habit of El Tigre to act before an idea grew stale. In the first bloom, the first fire of this thought, he stood up on his bough, measured his distance, and dropped.

The poor Hernando heard a slight whishing in the air above him and looked up as a pair of knees with a hundred and ninety pounds of weight behind them struck his shoulders close to each side of his face.

He fell without a groan. He lay like a rag while his uniform and boots were stripped from him. Half a minute or less, for that, with the powerful hands of Dallas handling the big coachman like a doll. The boots were easy. Dallas could simply step into them, and the uniform fitted quite well—a bit roomy about the belly and a bit tight across the shoulders.

There was still no sign of returning life in the coachman. And he, at least, would not find it easy to slip the bonds that were placed on him by Tom Dallas. He was fairly wired into a bundle and dragged into a nest of shrubbery. There he lay, his breathing slow and regular, his sleep very deep.

And now he was climbing into the driver's seat; now he was gathering the reins; now he was putting beside him, the barrel under his thigh, that old Colt that had seen him through so many perils. Even empty, it might be of immense use.

Porfilo appeared in haste, and took the leaders by the bits, calling out: "We wait for them at the front gate . . . the colonel, the *señorita*, and the damned *gringo!*"

That last was the word for Samuel Richmond, of course.

So Porfilo led the team around to the front gate and, coming back beside the driver's seat, murmured: "Hey, what doing . . . what a night of happenings . . . El Tigre . . . for the name of God, what a terrible man! What a flame."

Here he sprang to attention as the colonel came down the path with the girl and Sam Richmond. They were helped into the great open shell of the carriage—the colonel and the girl in the rear seat, Richmond facing them, his back to the driver. And now Porfilo sprang up to the driver's seat.

"To the fort!" called the colonel.

That meant through the town gate, and around the walls to the entrance of the fort. Through the town gate!

The horses were started by a word. A turn at stage-coaching had made Dallas a master of the reins as no other task in the world could have prepared him. Now he had swung the horses down the street when he heard a faint gasp from his companion.

"What are you?" muttered Porfilo.

"Name of heaven, these *are* the clothes of Hernando, but you. . . ."

"El Tigre!" Dallas hissed. And he could have laughed, such a wildness of triumph was coming up in his throat. "Be quiet. Give no alarm, and all goes well with you, *amigo*. Utter one word, and I smash your skull like a shell."

For answer, Porfilo turned up his eyes and began to mumble, softly, a prayer to the Virgin. He would make no move.

Before them loomed the tallest part of the wall, the great gate piercing it. A shout from the guard gave recognition to the colonel. They stood in a double rank presenting arms while the gate was dragged open—both the heavy panels, although one would have given ample room.

The colonel sang out as the carriage passed through: "Keep a watch for the devil tonight! He may appear!"

He was still laughing a little at his poor jest as the carriage issued onto the road that wound in two directions—one up toward the fort and in the other down a seven mile slant along the sloping side of a ravine. The whip sang, cracked flesh, and the four white horses stretched themselves in a trot, in a gallop down the lower slope.

"Name of a dog!" yelled the colonel in a terrible fury. "What? Are you drunk? I said the fort! The fort!"

Already they were shooting down the incline at a frightful speed. If they tampered with the driver now, they would be hurling themselves to sure death over a precipice hundreds of feet deep. And that was why Dallas merely laughed.

"What?" shouted the colonel. "Are you laughing? Are you drunk, Hernando?"

"Hernando is asleep in the garden!" shouted Dallas. "I am El Tigre!"

"It is true . . . El Tigre . . . God help me!" screamed the colonel. But he helped himself, for, seeing a thicket of brush close beside the road, he risked the thorns and broken bones by rising and hurling himself from the carriage into the air. The driver could not see the fall because he was reining in the near horses and flogging the off to take the carriage with a terrible skid around a sharp curve.

They rounded into a long, steady slant. Here he could risk a backward glance, and he saw that Samuel Richmond sat beside the girl in the rear seat, one arm steadying her and the other hand holding a naked revolver.

"Dallas!" he shouted. "Drive wherever you please . . . I have a bullet for you at the end of the drive!"

Well, that would be the answer to the trip, perhaps—for when

the road no longer followed the ravine, when the way was wide
and level and nothing serious was likely to happen if the stage
swerved from the road, then what would happen to the driver
from behind?

But the girl? She was not rigid and white as the moonlight,
like Sam Richmond. She was not a terrified pulp, like Porfilo;
she was crying out and laughing; she was rejoicing in every
careening lurch of that wild mad ride. Had he thought that only
he loved danger?

"Sally!" he called. "Now tell me the riddle! Tell me!"

He shouted the question, then yelled at the horses and shot
them around a horseshoe bend with the inner wheels both off
the ground for half the loop.

And there she was, standing up behind him, laughing:
"Faster, Tommy. Faster! There's no great riddle! I simply heard
Mister Gunman Richmond when he got the news of the death
of his worthless squawman brother. I heard him swear that he
would kill Tom Dallas. And why? Why would he have the guts
to hunt the man who had wrecked Los Gatos the year before?
Because he knew that Tom Dallas had not carried a bullet in his
gun for six months. That's why I came. . . ."

The voice of Richmond called: "Sally, come back here. Sit
down! You'll be thrown out in a minute! Sally, if you love
me. . . ."

"I despise you, you rat-brained murderer!" shouted Sally. "I
always *have* despised you. Tommy . . . darling . . . do you hear
me? I went to Spring Water to see what sort of a man would go
with an empty gun through a world filled with enemies. And I
saw you and I loved you, and I knew that you would never run
away from any man, even if your gun *was* empty. And then I
saw what I must do. I must put you away from danger even if I
had to put you into a jail. That was why I took you to Los Gatos. What else could I do?"

"Nothing!" thundered Dallas. "I understand it all. Sally, do you love me?"

"Yes!" cried the girl.

They scattered around a sharp curve. The off leader seemed to be stepping on air for an instant—the front off wheel was actually dipping through nothingness—but it jerked back onto the road.

"Kiss me!" called Sally.

And although another curve loomed, Dallas turned on the seat, caught her in his arm, and kissed her. The screaming of Porfilo was in his ear. The screeching of big Sam Richmond joined in it.

"Dallas . . . for God's sake, you'll murder us all!"

But Tom Dallas, laughing like a madman, stood up in his place and flogged the maddened horses down the slope while the stars trembled like candles in the wind of that galloping, and the loosened gravel and rocks spilled over the edge of the cliff and fell clattering and booming into the deadly chasm.

But the girl laughed, and so did Tom Dallas.

Sam Richmond, dropping his gun to grasp the seat with both hands, allowed the weapon to spill out over the side of the floor. He screamed again. He saw sharp, quick death before him and yelled again, closing his eyes—but around that turn there stretched the long levels of the valley floor, and the frightful danger was over.

"Take the reins!" called El Tigre to Porfilo, "and keep the horses at a gallop. I have a job that will lighten the carriage."

He passed the reins to the trembling hands of Porfilo as he spoke, and, whirling in his seat, flung himself straight back on Sam Richmond.

But there was no wildcat, struggling fight. Terror had robbed the body of Richmond of its power. He allowed himself to be lifted. For a moment he tried to cling, but a hard chopping fist that clipped the end of his chin relaxed all his muscles at once. He fell backward, clawed at the air. And then his scream of agony followed them down the road, for he had struck in the midst of a patch of cacti with fishhook claws.

"Drive on, and gallop 'em like the devil!" shouted Tom Dallas to Porfilo. "They'll never get tired because they're taking the two happiest people in the world on a long journey."

And so it seemed, for the white horses ran like the wind and never seemed ready to pause, while the girl and big Tom Dallas, lying in the arms of each other, drunken with delight waved to the wheeling moon and the stars above them.

"Sally, it was I that you said you would meet in Los Gatos. It was I that you said you loved."

"It was!" she cried.

"But if you love Tom Dallas . . . who was that other man? Who was the second man you loved? Tell me."

"El Tigre," she answered.

★ ★ ★ ★ ★

THE FIGHTING COWARD

★ ★ ★ ★ ★

"The Fighting Coward" was Frederick Faust's penultimate story to appear in Street & Smith's *Western Story Magazine,* the magazine with which he had an almost exclusive fifteen-year association, beginning in 1920. The story was published in the issue dated 1/26/35 under Faust's pen-name Hugh Owen. It is a tale of both mistaken identity and redemption. This is its first appearance since its original publication.

I

A single ray of light cut the darkness and showed nothing but the fingers of Bristol actively and accurately at work as he ran the mold of yellow laundry soap around the door of the safe. A dim image of the hands reflected in the steel.

"Chief!" called a voice that was half whisper, half murmur. "Hey, chief. Jack Bristol. Listen . . . the game's finished. We're cooked if we blow the safe. There's a dozen cowpunchers saddling up and getting ready to leave the hotel across the street. If we make a noise, they'll be over here in a jiffy. We gotta get out. We gotta leave this job for another time."

Bristol turned his head from his work, not to listen but because his work was ended with the running of the mold. He began to unwind a coil of slender fuse. The single ray of light, turning to follow his hands, slipped up and struck across his face. Once seen, the memory of it remained in the mind of the observer. It was the contrast that shocked the brain. Physically he was no more than twenty-two or twenty-three years of age, but the thin grip of the lips, set hard without straining, the perfect calm of the gray eyes, showed in him that strength of cold will that is found in old men alone.

"Chief, you hear me?" came the gasping whisper. "We gotta get out. The back way is still clear."

"Tucker," said the voice of Bristol, not at all lowered or muffled by imminent danger, "go back to the horses. Sandy, take the shake out of your hands. Steady that light."

A faint groan came from Tucker. "This time we'll be nabbed," he muttered.

But the order from his chief drove him back through the darkness. His last warning drifted faintly through the room.

"The day's almost here. It'll be dawn in a minute. The whole town'll be up."

Bristol turned his head and gave one swift glance toward the front. The big windows along the face of the bank were square blocks of translucent gray, now, and through them he could see the ragged roof line of the buildings across the street. Nearer at hand, the gilded steel bars of the various cages in the room had begun to shimmer faintly, like reflections in dusty mirrors. Out of the distance he heard voices, a man laughing, and then the trumpet sound of a neighing horse.

The town was rousing, no doubt, but he turned steadily back to his work. He moved quickly because he did all things quickly, because his touch was surer than the touch of other men, and because his hands moved instantly to execute his will.

Sandy, holding the dark lantern, allowed the thin ray that struck from it to shudder with the shaking of his arm.

"Look, chief," he said. "Look. We can't do it. It's a tough town. If they catch us, they'll lynch us all. It's a tough bunch of *hombres* around here."

Bristol said nothing.

He stood up, took out a small glass flask, and began to pour the thick, pale liquid it contained into the orifice at the top of the mold. The work required whole minutes. The breathing of Sandy became more and more noisy.

"If your nerve's leaving you, get out and stay out and never let me see your mug again," said Bristol as he finished the pouring. He added gently: "The soup never worked better than it's going to work this time."

He made his last arrangements quickly, lighted the end of the fuse, and only then covered the face of the safe with some quilts and blankets that were heaped on the floor.

The running, sparkling, spitting fire of the fuse ran over the floor and was near the safe before Bristol calmly turned, went to a corner of the room, and lay down on his face. Through the noise of the burning fuse, he could hear a faint groan made with every breath that Sandy drew. And beyond—in that safe outer world—he heard more men laughing, distantly, and the thin jingling of saddle trappings.

Well, those were the fellows who lived inside the law. They were the sheep who huddled together for strength. He considered them cruel, cowardly, selfish, weak except in numbers, and he despised them a little more than he despised the members of his band who lived outside the law not because they loved glorious freedom but because they hated labor. If the men inside the law were sheep, his own followers were wolves. He scorned them even as he used them.

The noise of the spitting fuse ended. There was a deep, breathless interval of silence, and then the explosion came. It was like the beating together of gigantic, hollowed palms. It was a thick puff of wind; there was no crack or clang. He felt an instant's pressure all over his body. And then he heard a second noise—a jarring fall.

Was that the door of the safe falling out on the blankets and quilts that had helped to muffle the noise of the shot?

He ran quickly. Sandy, in terror, was shooting the ray of his lantern from a distance, and it showed Bristol the door on the floor, and the inner face of the safe open, naked, set across with its little rows of steel boxes.

Bristol set to work on them with a can opener. They ripped out one after the other. They might almost as well have been made of pasteboard, when an expert attacked them.

The voice of Sandy stammered, groaning: "Chief, come on

away. Chief! They're coming . . . they're here . . . twenty of 'em."

"Get out," commanded Bristol. "Leave that light, and get out of here, you yellow hound."

He gave one glance over his shoulder. In the quickening daylight he could see men swarming out from the alley that ran past the hotel toward the stable behind it. Those fellows were cowpunchers and they were armed, nearly every man. Moreover, they were able to use their weapons.

Sandy, hesitating, finally dropped to one knee. Each breath he drew was a gasp; each breath he exhaled was a faint moan. He was in mortal terror of his life, but he seemed to be in still greater fear of his chief. But this appeared to be the exquisite, the perfect moment, for Bristol. His thin nostrils quivered and expanded. A very small smile worked at the corners of his mouth, and his eyes were flashing. Life was now perfect for him because his hold on the future was so slight. No connoisseur of music or of perfumes or of beauty could have expressed such perfect joy as this silent passion of Jack Bristol.

He worked on very rapidly, removing the small drawers, bent and thrust from the hold of their locks, and emptying their contents into a capacious canvas sack.

A hand rapped at the front door of the bank. Then it was rattled loudly.

"Hello inside!" shouted a voice.

Against the dim morning light, those figures were black silhouettes pasted against the glass of the windows.

"It's enough . . . we got the bulk of it," murmured the voice of Sandy. "Come on, chief. They'll be here in a second."

Enough? It was not enough when one scruple of the loot remained behind, unsecured. "Thorough" was the motto of Jack Bristol. He was thorough now, emptying the last of the drawers at the same time that a revolver butt shattered the glass

75

of the front door.

A hand reached through and turned the latch on the inside. The door was thrust open, and entering feet crunched heavily, loudly over the fallen glass that strewed the floor.

"All right, Sandy," said his chief at last, rising from his knees.

Yet he looked around him with a certain regret. It was not his way to leave the scene of a crime so untidy. Usually all tools were carried away, and even the blankets should at least have been folded, for he was possessed by a truly feminine sense of neatness and order.

Sandy was gliding before him, crouched close to the floor, stepping off in a nervous panic now that his chief had released him from the dreadful vigil. But Jack Bristol followed more slowly, erect, stepping smoothly.

Perhaps that was why they saw him.

Suddenly a fellow shouted: "Who's there? What's that?"

Well, they would rush, the next second. But Bristol gave them something to chew on before they charged.

"It's Jack Bristol!" he thundered. "Come on and take me. Come on to get famous, boys! Here I am!"

He dodged back through a rear door and heard from behind him the explosion of half a dozen guns, the crashing of the bullets into the wall, the outcry of a number of enraged or frightened voices.

But there was no thundering forward rush of footfalls. They were not closing in blindly on Jack Bristol. That knowledge gave him a keen, quick, deep thrust of pleasure.

They were sheep . . . his men were wolves . . . and what was he? He could not have suggested an answer to that.

Over his head and shoulders he dropped a hood of black cloth that covered him as far as the elbows. A strong elastic held the mask in place over his face, hiding his features. And so he stepped out into the alley behind the bank.

Sandy and Tucker were already in the saddle, bent forward, ready to fly, but Tucker still held the reins of the big gray gelding, Duster. For years Jack Bristol had ridden where fortune tempted him to go. And for four years Duster had been his luck and had carried him safely through every escape. Age or a well-aimed bullet would stop the gray gelding one day.

Bristol caught the reins that Tucker threw and swung into the saddle, hooking the canvas bag over the pommel.

"Down the Townsend Draw," he commanded. "I'll go back through the north pass. You know where to meet."

The pair was off in a flash, using their spurs deeply, bending to cut through the air.

Inside the bank came the rush of the footfalls, at last. A gun barked and knocked a little hole in a window—a small round eye in the glass, with long cracks extending from it through the height and breadth of the pane.

There was battering on the rear door, which Bristol had locked as he came through, but, as the door crashed wide, Duster was under way, and gathering speed.

Around the next corner they swerved to the right, then left, then right again, with the depth of the dust muffling the footfalls. They could trail him, perhaps, by the dust that was kicked up by the digging hoofs of the horse, but, with the wind that was blowing, this evidence would not last for long.

He had good hopes of getting away clear from the start, but then he heard a screeching voice that seemed to come out of the middle of the sky, crying: "There he goes on the north trail! There he goes!"

He looked back. A gray-headed woman was leaning out of an upper window of the hotel. She screamed like an eagle.

He had always hated women. Now he felt there was a peculiar justification for his dislike.

II

The yelling voice of the old woman kept a strain in the mind of Jack Bristol until he was at the top of the first hill north of the town of New Eden. Then, looking back, he saw a swarm of six, a dozen, a score of riders who issued in a long stream and took after him. The greatness of his amusement made him wish to laugh; the greatness of his scorn silenced him.

Sheep running, shaking their heads, bleating, throwing up their foolish heels. Well, they would never catch gray Duster. He turned to rush the long-legged horse forward and found himself confronting a tall, brown-faced young man with a dog at his side and a shotgun in his hands.

Here, from triumph, at a stroke he was brought to desperation.

"Stick 'em up!" snapped the stranger.

Bristol pushed his hands at once above his head. With a touch of his left heel, he pushed his horse toward the right, toward the man of the shotgun. That was what made the difference—the shotgun. He could take chances with any other weapon, but the shotgun gripped too much space—it would not miss. In the sidling movement of his horse, there was a ghost of a hope that he might be brought close enough to achieve something.

The stranger stepped back.

"Keep the horse back, too," he said. "Wait a minute. By the look of that black hood and the gray of your horse I'd say that you're Bristol, eh? Jack Bristol . . . the great Bristol, eh?"

"I am," said Jack Bristol, and, instead of moving his gelding away, with a pressure of his unseen knee and a touch of the same spur, he made the gray swing suddenly with its forehead toward the man of the shotgun.

The fellow was quick enough. He leaped away from the heavy head of the gelding, but Bristol's reaching foot struck out from the saddle and knocked the muzzles of the gun straight up.

They roared into the air, and Bristol looked down the barrel of a Colt into the astonished face of the stranger.

He was amazed to hear the other cry out: "Good work, Bristol! I wondered what the devil you'd do then. I thought I had you!"

The whole life of Bristol came to a pause. He had never known anything like this. This was apparently neither sheep nor wolf. The eye of the man was very open, very clear, very blue. He was tall, and there was a splendid strength in his carriage, and a nobility in the way his head was set on his shoulders. But here he was, smiling fearlessly into the leveled revolver of an outlaw!

"Go on and get away from 'em, Bristol," said the stranger. "By the time I'm loaded, you'll be out of danger from me. And I know that you don't shoot unarmed men. Away with you, and ride like the devil, now, or else they'll start peppering you at long range with their rifles."

"Who are you?" asked Bristol.

"Tom Reardon. So long, Jack."

Bristol did the strangest thing he had ever attempted in his strange life. He slipped his gun into his left hand and held out his right. It was instantly and heartily gripped.

"I understand," said Reardon. "It's not the money that you want, but a chance to lead the right sort of life. I understand . . . and so long, Jack!"

The gray carried Bristol like the wind down the hill and into a straggling copse. Through a gap in the trees he looked back and saw the posse from the town of New Eden rushing up to Reardon on the hilltop, where he waved them with energy in the wrong direction, down the right-hand way that plunged into more distant trees, also.

Bristol went on at his leisure.

He had never had a friend in his life, but he wanted the

friendship of Reardon. The blue eyes of the man seemed to shine on him still and with a light that penetrated to his heart. And the smile of Reardon was open and frank, unlike the smiling of any other men he'd ever known, hypocritical men, trying to hide the real meanings of their minds.

Who was Tom Reardon? He had been dressed like any hard-working ranch hand, out for a few hours of fun with a gun and a dog. But in the life of Bristol, he was a marked man.

He was young, this Reardon. He was in his early twenties. How could he have lived long enough to gain that quality that had endeared him suddenly to Bristol?

The outlaw rode on with a furrow between his eyes, and a faint smile on his lips. The brown of the mountains was a richer, more golden color; the blue of distance was a deeper velvet. A purer wind blew the unseen river of the sky, and the world was subtly altered.

In that sense of difference he rode all the way through the north pass and then into the tangled wilderness, the hole-in-the-wall country where, for three years, he had kept his camp. Many a posse had entered that region of criss-cross ravines, dense pine woods, and mountains where every second trail had to bend and twist along the sides of streams that were unfordable during most of the year. No man could know those mountains from a map, because according to the weather they were penetrable or impassable. Sometimes in the winter the blizzards froze them white; sometimes in the summer the thunderstorms washed out sections from the most valued trails. It was only to men who lived constantly among these mountains beyond the north pass that travel through them was fairly simple. For this reason, Bristol had kept his crew of outlaws from any devastating vengeance during these years. He had enabled them to live on the fat of the land, and the efforts of the law had fallen astray, like gestures made furiously in the dark.

When he came toward the present camp, he had to urge the gray through a narrow defile that twisted like a snake between rocky walls. He was near the mouth of this narrow place before a voice hailed him.

"Hey, chief! What's been up?"

A red-skinned, freckled man looked over the top of a rock. The freckles appeared like small sores in the flesh.

"Nothing much," answered Bristol, and patted the canvas bag in which the loot was stored.

Sandy and Tucker had been given a shorter way home, but they had not yet appeared to spread the good news of the raid through the camp. Perhaps they had been snagged on the way. He would not care, greatly, if they were caught and finished, fighting. But if they were jailed, he would have to get them out. That was always his principle: to demand blind, scrupulous obedience, to punish every fault with severity, but to share all profits equitably, and to keep his men from the grip of the law.

The narrows opened and let him have a look into a deep and widening prospect of a rounded valley. Small, dark peninsulas of trees invaded the brightness of the grass lands, and several old shacks, spotted here and there, the homes of prospectors or of vanished squatters, offered a ready-made nucleus for the camp. To the west there was a tall precipice with the blue white of a waterfall arching down across its face. The voice of this falling water sounded constantly through the valley. The stream worked in quick curves across the open and disappeared into the eastern cleft that made the second approach to the camp.

This perfect little spot for seclusion needed no fortification. A guard in each of the narrow ways that led into the place adequately secured it against a surprise attack. And for food, they had a herd of selected beef, a flock of very good sheep, and a number of goats. These animals were confined without the need of a fence to hold them. This natural confinement offered them ample food and water, and the home of the Bristol crowd was also its wide larder.

Jack Bristol, as he looked down on the big amphitheater, was aware not for the first time of the perfect choice that he had made. Then he jaunted the gray slowly down the slope toward the central cabin, which was his. The men slept in the old shacks on the right and the left of this. Therefore, he was surprised when he heard voices issuing through his door.

He listened only for a moment. Then he unsaddled the gray and turned him loose. Carrying the saddle and the bulky saddlebag, he stepped into his doorway.

The whole crew was in there, six of them gathered for a poker game, and three more lounging, looking on.

When his shadow fell inward, across the floor, Scotty looked up and suddenly rose to his feet with a groan.

"The chief!"

They whirled to their feet and cowered. The calm glance of Bristol found instantly the one spot of danger. That was Sid Lester, tall, powerful, with eyes so small that they were jeweled spots of brilliance in his face.

The man was a killer, and he looked like a killer now. The rest of the crew was simply frightened.

"Why jump and cringe like a lot of calves when a dog barks?" asked Sid Lester.

He stood by the end of the table, his right hand hovering over his holster, ready for the draw. The rest of the crew backed away toward the walls, toward the doorway that Bristol had left empty.

"You got the only decent table in the valley," said Sid Lester. "Why ain't we got the right to use it, eh?"

Bristol walked across the room, slowly, letting his saddle and the thick canvas bag slump to the floor. He flicked the back of his left hand across the face of Lester. The hard knuckles made a loud, cracking sound against the flesh. And a beading of blood appeared across the killer's mouth.

Lester remained half crouched, his little eyes glittering against the eyes of Bristol. In this manner he endured for a moment. Then his glance wandered. He stuck out his tongue and licked the blood from his lips. Slowly, with a thoughtful air, and still with his body bent a little, he walked across the floor and left the cabin.

The others squeezed out suddenly behind his back. The grass rustled under their feet. Only at a distance did their guarded voices begin to sound.

And Bristol sneered as he heard them.

Every now and again he had to crack the whip to remind them that he was master. Every now and again one of them would dare to face him for an instant with murder ready and prepared. But not one of them could confront him for more than a moment.

He pulled open the crazy, groaning window at the side of the house and let the wind blow through. He felt that his quarters had been polluted.

III

Sandy and big Tucker appeared a few hours later. They came to the door of the chief's cabin and talked to him as he lay stretched on a bunk with a roll of blankets to raise his head. He could see a wedge of dark pines climbing the southern slope of the valley. A pair of young bulls had been threatening each other, pawing up clots of the green turf, blowing their wrath over the scars they left in the ground. Above, the ragged top of the mountain jutted into that tremendous distance of blue sky that he was never tired of looking at. Through a school window he had first stared at it, lost profoundly. Now, like familiar music, it always brought back the first, childish happiness.

Sandy was saying: "You called it pretty fine, today, but you done the trick, all right. Like you always do. How much is there in the sack, chief?"

"I don't know. We don't split it up till the first of the month. You know that," said Bristol.

"So you ain't even counted it?" demanded Tucker, on a rising note.

"We heard a rumor over on the Seven Pines," said Sandy, "that there was forty thousand in that haul."

"Yeah? That's all right," said Bristol. "Back up and get out of the view, will you?"

They backed up and got out of the view. Silent snarls were carved into their faces, but he cared nothing about snarls as long as they were not audible. He knew what the men said when they were together. Growling softly, they swore to one another that they would not endure the tyranny of their master any longer. They would put an end to his rule. They would lay him on his back, one day, with lead in his heart.

That was their talk. But talk did not bother Bristol. Sometimes he told himself that he would not have enjoyed life so much if there had not been constant danger to handle. Unless the coal is hot, it need not be handled with swift fingers—and it will never start a fire. These fellows all had enough of the savage heat in them. They could make flames, well and good. And that was all he demanded of them, in the final analysis. He would simply teach the fire where to burn.

Now they could retire to their fellows and snarl.

He had two perfect days, the sort that he liked the most. It was always after some exploit, when he began to gather ideas for his next foray, and while his body rested passively, that he found a singular peace and quiet of thought. And it was during these times that ideas would begin to grow up little by little, forming from day to day, slowly. Each hour added little to the height, but in a week the tree had grown to the full and was pointing its dizzy top among the stars.

And he wanted, on this occasion, something new. He wanted to try a thing he had never tried before, something that might tax all the strength of his wits and the hands of his band. Some of them had been too idle for too long.

He had never stopped a train. The thought intrigued him. The smoke blown sloping back over the train, like wild hair, and the thunder of power over the rails, and then the scream of the brakes, and the stilling of all that power, and the strange, deep-throated murmur of many people coming from the passenger coaches, and the cursing of the fireman as he turned in water through the fire box—he had never been present at a scene like this. Why should he not create one, then?

This thought had not taken full possession of his mind on the second day. It was simply a process of rootage, the thought working deeper and deeper into his mind. And he was lying in the warmth of the middle afternoon under a tree, half in sunshine and half in the damp cool of the shadow, when Butch, the freckled fellow whose face always looked raw, came to him and leaped panting from his horse.

"There's a woman . . . ," he said.

His panting interrupted him—also the voice of the chief saying: "There's no woman for me. What the devil do you mean?"

"Up there," said Butch. "Up there in the mouth of the pass. She's beggin' to see you."

"Tell her that I can't be seen."

"Wait a minute, chief. You've seen a lot of others, but you never seen one like this."

"Like a picture, is she?" The chief sneered.

"No," said Butch, earnestly scratching his head in the confusion of his thought, "she ain't like a picture. She's like the print that goes under one of the pictures. Print of big words that are hard to read."

"I'm not reading, today," said the chief. "Send her away."

"Well, I'll send her, then," said Butch unwillingly. "She said to tell you that her name was Reardon."

"Reardon?" exclaimed the chief, and leaped to his feet. "Reardon, did you say?"

"Kate Reardon, is what she said."

"Up there in the south pass?"

"Yes."

Bristol leaped on the pinto that Butch had ridden down and plunged the tough mustang straight up the slope. The gelding was wheezing and heaving before it came into the throat of the pass, and there Bristol saw a slender girl in tan riding clothes, talking with Sid Lester.

"Well," said Lester, "he *is* coming. I never thought the chief would do that for a woman."

Bristol swung down from the saddle. He did not have to stare at her in order to get the picture well in his mind. She was not like her brother. Her eyes were sea-green, rather than blue. She was not tall. It was only in the proud, fearless carriage of her head that she resembled Tom Reardon.

Bristol lifted his hat to her. "Give us some room," he said to Sid Lester.

The fellow took the order with a poisonous gleam of hate in his eyes. But he gave way at once and left them out of earshot.

"You *are* Jack Bristol?" she asked him.

"That's what I'm called," he said. "Did you expect something else?"

Perhaps she was not the sister of Tom Reardon. Merely a cousin, he guessed.

"I expected a gray horse," she said.

"And a black mask?" asked Bristol.

She smiled a little. The smile seemed unwilling to stay on her lips, and it left them at once.

"You *are* Jack Bristol," she decided, "and that means I have to talk to you."

He waited.

"My brother met you the other day on the trail out of New Eden. He came home and talked a good deal about that meeting. You set him on fire. I suppose you set most men on fire?"

He met the cold, calm challenge of the question without an answer.

After a pause, she went on. "That fire burned his own hands. We're a poor family. Tommy decided that he'd lift the debts at one whack. He went out and stuck up the Mud Flat stage. To make sure that he didn't hurt anyone, he didn't load his revolver."

"And they grabbed him?"

"He's in the New Eden jail," said the girl.

"Well, what of it?" asked Bristol.

She looked him over. She had extraordinary eyes. They spoke more than her voice. He could see the thought, and the passing shadow of judgment in them.

"I thought you might want to know," she answered.

"I'm sorry about him," answered the outlaw. "But that's all I am . . . sorry."

She nodded.

"He tried his hand and he lost. Prison will give him a chance at a lot of second thoughts, and maybe he'll come out and take a second chance," suggested the hard voice of Bristol.

He waved his hand down the pass. "If you want to get out of the mountains before it's dark, you'd better be starting along," he told her.

"Are you the man that shook hands with Tom Reardon?" she asked.

"What of it?" he said, frowning. "What do I owe him?"

"Owe him?" she exclaimed. "Nothing! Nothing! I didn't come here to ask to have a debt paid."

She waved her hand at him hastily.

"I'll be sloping along," she said, and with that put her foot in the stirrup and swung on the back of a good, tough-looking bay mare. *"¡Adiós!"* she called over her shoulder.

Whatever was in her mind, she made herself smile, and the smile did something to the chief. It took hold of his heart and twisted all the strings with a strange pain.

"Wait a minute!" he called.

"Well?" she said, pulling up the mustang.

He walked up to her and stood at the shoulder of her horse, looking up into her face. It was a little too thin. Pain had stiffened her lips a trifle and shadowed her eyes. She needed more laughter in her life, more ease and jollity. If she had that, she would be a shining beauty. But the years had cast a dust over her. He marveled to find himself pursuing these thoughts.

"You wanted to say something?" asked the girl at last.

He started. How long had he been staring up at her, thinking his thoughts?

"I shook hands with Tom Reardon," he said. "I liked him better than any other man that I ever met. What about it?"

She was nodding at him. "It's like this," she said. "Tom thought that just the look of a man in a long black hood and riding a gray horse would be enough to freeze the blood and stop the hands of ordinary people. And down there in New Eden they think that they have the real Jack Bristol in the jail. He went out, like a silly fool, and rode a gray horse and was caught. The same sort of a horse and the same sort of a hood that *you* were wearing. The people in New Eden are a happy lot, just now."

"Happy?" exclaimed Bristol. "Do you know what they'll do? They'll lynch him as sure as there's a sky over our heads. They'll lynch him."

"Yes," said the girl as calmly as before. "They'll lynch him about nightfall of today."

IV

After this, the outlaw squinted toward the edge of the sky. There is a thin gap between the blue of the heavens and the dark of the earth. It is a stroke of radiance that divides the two and into which the eye can travel forever. Bristol seemed to be gathering meanings. But he could not tell what it was that was working so in his blood. He had pity for Tom Reardon, but it was as nothing compared with the strange, cold anguish that he felt when he looked at the pain in the face of this girl and the exquisite willpower with which she controlled her trouble.

Bristol called to Sid Lester, and the killer stalked forward.

"Go down into the valley as fast as you can spur, and saddle Duster and bring him back with you," Bristol directed. "But, first, step inside my shack and take the striped canvas sack off the wall. Bring that with you."

"You mean the stuff . . . ?" began Lester.

"Don't ask me what I mean. Do what I tell you to do," said Bristol.

Sid Lester stared, turned, mounted the pinto, and rode at a furious rate through the mouth of the pass. He was torturing the flanks of his mount with the spurs.

"That man will try to murder you, someday," said the girl.

"Will he?" asked Bristol absently. "This brother of yours, how old is he?"

"Twenty-three."

"Has he always gone straight?"

"Straight as a string."

The outlaw looked up and saw a long-winged hawk sweeping through the air, swimming across the great blue bowl of the sky. *There* was freedom.

"I understand," said Bristol. He said not a word more except: "I'm going back. I'll get your brother out."

"Get him out? How?" she asked.

He did not seem to hear. He walked up and down, slowly, lost in his thought. He had never imagined that a human being would be able to exercise over him a claim so strong as this. But Tom Reardon had that power. It was the supreme folly of the imitation that he had made—perhaps that was what moved Bristol so much.

A black hood, a gray horse—and an empty gun!

Bristol could have laughed, but curses were closer to his teeth than laughter.

Sid Lester came back with the gray horse on the lead. The bag of striped canvas hung from the pommel of the saddle.

"Some of the boys would like to ask . . . ," began Lester.

"What do they want to ask?" demanded Bristol.

"Aw . . . nothing," drawled Lester.

"Sid," said the chief, "there's a lot of room in these mountains. Why don't you take a trip and stay away?"

"Are you firing me?" asked Lester.

"I never fire any man," said Bristol. "But you know what I mean. Do as you please . . . go or stay. I'm only telling you . . . there's a lot of room in the mountains."

Sid Lester said nothing at all, and his chief mounted and rode down the narrows of the pass at the side of the girl.

Once, she turned and looked sharply back, then she rode on again, shivering slightly.

"Was Lester handling a rifle?" asked the chief.

"How did you guess?" asked the girl.

"If you stay in the cage with tigers long enough, you know when they're hungry for raw meat," answered Bristol, and he laughed a little, quite cheerfully.

They talked very little. Now and again he looked toward the west, estimating the distance that lay between them and the town of New Eden, and the time it would take for the sun to sink. There seemed to be a sufficient space to let him enter the town. And it was unlikely that a mob would rise before darkness came.

They had just crossed a ford and were climbing the farther bank, brilliantly a-drip with water, when the girl said: "You can't go masked into a crowd, can you?"

"No," he said.

"And if you don't wear a mask, someone is apt to know your face?"

"Maybe."

That was all she said about it. No protesting. No false movements or wasting of words, whatever. She had come to find a man who might risk his life to save her brother. She had found such a man. Why should she either mourn or exclaim over him?

Bristol liked this silent honesty.

Afterward, when they came out on the brow of the hills, and the wide sweep of the land descended toward the glimmering windows of the town of New Eden, and the shadows of its streets, she said: "I haven't a right to ask . . . but, if you have so many men, couldn't you use them in work like this?"

"I can spend them trying to get what they want," answered Bristol. "They want money, or a good time. I don't mind seeing them drop at that sort of work. But this time I'm doing something for myself."

She had to squint her eyes and look far off before she could understand this sort of even-handed justice. But, as before, she was silent as soon as she saw the point.

She made only one more speech to him, and that was when, on the top of a lower knoll, he said to her abruptly: "You go your way. I've come close enough with you, now."

Then she exclaimed: "Will you try to use me, in some way? I don't care how. To hold a stirrup . . . or to hold a gun . . . I don't care. I'll do anything!"

"Break the law?" he answered, gripping his teeth hard together as he looked at her. "Would you do that, too? Would you break the law?"

"Yes," she answered.

"Aye," said the outlaw. "There's something that's right and decent in that brother of yours. But . . . so long."

An excitement had come into his voice as he looked at her. He banished it, and made the last phrase calm and emotionless. Then he let the long-legged gray step in a rolling lope down the road toward New Eden.

He wanted to look back at her at least once, but he checked this impulse, also. A singular fear had crept into his blood. He knew that men fall when they yield to weakening instincts. Many a wolf has been caught by first trapping its mate. And what might this girl become to him, one day?

He put the thought behind him resolutely. It was not true that she had entered his heart. It was only that she, of all women in the world, was something more than an unpleasant blank to him.

He was puzzled. It was not that she attracted him so much. It was the fear that she might attract him in the future. And what would she be if the starved look left her and he could see the flowering of her beauty?

The sun sank as he rode into New Eden.

V

He went around the outer streets of the dusty little town, in a circle. There were no gatherings except toward the center of New Eden, and above all near the big hotel that held, in its wings, the best saloon, the biggest grocery store, and the leading barbershop of New Eden.

In that saloon the people milled in a steadily increasing jam. By the tones in which men called for whiskey, Bristol knew the signs of rising temper.

Under the open window of the saloon he halted his gray horse. Men have to have leaders before they can accomplish anything. And for evil purposes leaders are found far more readily than for good. On this occasion there arose in the crowd a budding orator. He was a lean-faced young man with a great deal of nose. He had long, lank, black hair, and a very large, very flexible mouth. Above all, he had a voice that could bellow one moment and sink to gentle murmurs the next.

His name was Cal Thompson. Cal saw his opportunity and was seizing it by the forelock. He had no better rostrum than a chair, but he stood on this and waved one arm like the baton of a presiding officer.

"Gents," said Cal Thompson, "gimme a chance to talk a minute, will you? Ladies and gents. . . ."

"There ain't any ladies here," said a joker.

This brought a bawling burst of laughter. Mirth turned all attention to Cal. He should have been crushed. Instead, he was a man to seize on this and make a golden chance of it, also. For he cried: "Yes, it's for the women that we gotta do the thinkin' . . . *and* the fightin', now! What sort of men have we looked when Jack Bristol was ridin' the roads and murderin' his victims . . . ?"

"Bristol's no murderer!" broke in a voice.

"He is!" shouted several others. "Him or his men . . . it's all one."

"He ain't any murderer," persisted a voice. "He'll flay any of his gang that uses a gun till he has to."

"Leave murder out," said Cal loudly. "It's for the honor and the name of New Eden that we had oughta take this job in hand. I want to call your attention to something. Over there in the jail the robber is sittin' pretty, drinkin' coffee, smokin' cigarettes, and all the time sure that, when his case comes up in court, he'll get out of this snag. Why is he sure? Because he has plenty of money to hire lawyers. Understand what I mean? Out of the loot that he grabbed from our bank, he's got enough money to buy up any court in this land. You know what money does. You seen it in the newspapers, plenty. Here is the law, on one side, and it says that it's goin' to take its time with the punishin' of Mister Jack Bristol. And on the other hand, here is the town of New Eden, the people of the town, and they say that they don't want no time wasted. They won't stand for it."

A big, fat man at the bar began to beat his hand on the wood till it resounded like a drum.

"Go it, Cal!" he shouted.

"Go it! Tell us what to do!" called someone else.

Fire filled the eyes of Cal Thompson. He threw out both his arms and shouted: "There ain't but one thing to do, and that's to take Jack Bristol out of the jail and to hang him to the highest tree in the town! We'll show the law what sort of red-blooded folks we are in this town! We'll make every bad man or boy shake in his boots when he even hears the name of our town. We'll. . . ."

Here he was drowned out, for a moment, by a brief, angry roar of determination from the crowd.

There was another interruption a second later when a striped canvas bag was flung through the open window. It struck the eloquent Cal Thompson full in the face, staggered him off his chair, and recoiled at the feet of the leading butcher of New Eden.

He picked it up and jerked open the mouth of the bag.

Other men in the saloon were turning in rage toward the open window through which the bag had been thrown. They were in no humor to have practical jests played on them. But before they could explore the dark of the night immediately outside the window, they heard the butcher utter a strange cry that might have been caused by either pain or joy.

"It's money!" he shouted. "It's all money inside. But listen to this."

He read aloud from a bit of paper that was tied to the mouth of the bag:

Don't hang an honest man for being Jack Bristol. Reardon tried to play a joke. Rather than have him sent up for things he didn't do, I'm returning the stuff I got out of the New Eden bank.

The signature to this odd note was *Jack Bristol,* and, when the name was read out loud, it brought a great shouting from the men in the saloon.

People went off at once to find the banker and bring him there where he could receive his money in front of the crowd.

Outside the window, still lingering there where he could listen and watch, Jack Bristol peered at the confusion of the crowd and heard the strange workings of the mob mind.

The saloonkeeper was beating on the bar and exclaiming: "This here is a thing worth noticing, gents! Here's a crook gives up forty, fifty thousand dollars. Gives that money up to save a gent that's wearing the wrong name. Think that over, and it sounds pretty good."

It *did* sound good to the men of New Eden. There were plenty of compliments to Jack Bristol in the air when the banker came into the room. He was a tall, leaning man, who habitually smiled down at the ground. When he looked up, the smile vanished, the eyes became hard. He was only of middle age, but he had the body angle of age.

He was not a popular fellow, as a rule, but now the men made room for him and called for a speech.

He held the canvas sack gripped under his left arm, like a recovered child pressed close to his breast. He merely said: "I'm grateful in a way to all of you people. You put on the pressure that made Mister Jack Bristol afraid another man was going to be hanged in his place. I never heard of a fellow, before this day, so anxious to keep another man from using the rope that he ought to be stretching himself. I thank Mister Tom Reardon . . . I thank Mister Jack Bristol . . . I thank you all."

This speech brought a good deal of laughter, and before the mirth had ended, the banker was gone from the saloon, which he had never entered before.

It seemed that the mob that had gathered to hang Tom Reardon might break up in general drunkenness and good nature, but Cal Thompson did not wish to give up an audience so fitted to his hand. He wanted to impress himself on the minds of his fellow townsmen. Therefore he climbed back on a chair and shouted until he got the ear of the crowd again.

Then he said: "Gentlemen, I hope you see what you're doin'. I hope you see that you're barkin' up the wrong tree. I hope that you'll listen to me for a minute."

"Go ahead, Cal," someone sang out. "Warm yourself up and make us another speech. You can keep on talkin' as long as the whiskey lasts."

Cal Thompson went on, after the chuckling had died away.

"You take it that this here money comes from the real Jack Bristol, but that's where you're all wrong."

Outside the window, Jack Bristol blinked a little. He listened more carefully as the energetic Cal went on, surrounded now by a curious silence.

"I ask you, one and all, would a fellow like Jack Bristol give a damn because another gent is gonna be hanged in his place?"

He waited with a raised hand, as though waiting for answers, but long before the answers could be given, he had sailed ahead with his speech.

"What we know about Jack Bristol is that he's as cold as steel. He wouldn't care if a hundred men was to up and die in his place. He'd only laugh. And now I ask you . . . would a fellow like Jack Bristol go and part himself from forty thousand dollars for the sake of another man?"

"You answer the riddle, Cal?" called a voice.

"Here's the answer," said Cal Thompson. "It ain't Bristol that's sent in the money. It's Bristol's men!"

"Hey, how can you make that out?" called one.

"Ain't it easy to prove that Jack Bristol is really Neighbor Tom Reardon?" asked Cal Thompson. "After the bank was robbed, didn't the boys run into Reardon right spang in the middle of the trail they were chasin' along? He didn't have no horse with him, then. He had a shotgun and a dog, mighty innocent. Why? Because one of his crooks was out there and met him and gave him the gun and the dog, and took his horse and rode along. And then Reardon showed the boys the wrong trail to follow, and they caught nothing. Slick and easy, I call that. But it was too easy. It was so easy that Reardon thought he'd try his hand with the stage . . . and there he was caught with his gray horse and his long black hood, and all. Ain't it clear that Reardon is Jack Bristol?"

There was a silence, then a murmur of indistinct voices.

Cal went on: "Now, boys, look at the thing this way, will you? We've caught Jack Bristol, and we've got him in jail . . . under the real name of Reardon. And then what happens? Bristol's gang put their heads together. They've been living easy for years because they've had a leader. They say to themselves that it's better to give up the loot from the New Eden bank than it is to give up their leader. So they throw back this sack of money and they send the note along with it and pretend that the money comes from the real Jack Bristol."

As he made this point, a sudden howl of understanding and anger came from the men in the saloon.

"Now, you listen to me!" went on Cal Thompson, shouting in his triumph, expanding in his glory. "If we don't do something, Bristol-Reardon is going to get out of our hands. Forty thousand dollars has been spent tonight to turn him loose. There'll be a hundred thousand more to spend on the heels of this to set him free if ever he comes up for trial. What are we gonna do about it? Well, we're gonna see that he gets what's comin' to him this very night. We got the brains to see through the tricks of the crooks. We got the hands to break open the jail. We got the ropes that'll hang Mister Jack Bristol-Reardon."

He paused, and there was a growling answer that meant more than any shouting.

"There's only one question," went on Cal Thompson. "When do we start?"

"Now!" shouted a score of voices.

The listener outside the window had heard enough. He turned his horse and rode quickly away out of the trees that had screened him. Down the next lane he passed, and paused at a hitch rack to untether a good-looking, tall horse that was standing, head down, outside its master's house. In a copse of big brush and small trees behind the jail, Bristol left both horses and went around to the front of the jail.

He pulled his wide-brimmed sombrero down over his face a little and beat on the door of the jail. For answer, a small shutter in the door was opened. A broad ray of lantern light issued and struck him over the head and shoulders.

"Yeah?" demanded a voice.

"I'm a friend of Tom Reardon," said Bristol. "The mob's getting together to lynch him. Where's the sheriff?"

"I'm the sheriff."

"You Sheriff Dolan?"

"Yes."

"What're you going to do to save Reardon from that gang?"

"What *can* I do?"

"Let me in and I'll help you, Dolan. I'll help you fight 'em off."

"You mean you'll help to pump lead into the people of New Eden? I wouldn't scratch the finger of an honest man to save the neck of a crook like Reardon, or Bristol, or whatever his name is."

"Wait a minute. . . ."

"I've waited too long!" exclaimed the sheriff, and slammed the shutter.

Bristol turned slowly from the door. He heard, out of the distance, a sudden moaning, mournful sound larger than could have come from a single throat, and he knew that it was the growl of the crowd as it poured from the saloon and passed into the open air.

There were not many minutes left, if Bristol were to perform his promise to the girl and get Reardon out of the jail.

He had been in the hands of that brown-faced, handsome, smiling fellow. Those hands had easily opened and let him go. But would not any other man have sent a double charge of buckshot into the outlaw and claimed the glory and the head money afterward?

It was not ordinary for Bristol to owe anything to other men. He gave from carelessness or deep purpose; he took by force.

But he never owed thanks to others. That was why he was baffled, half choked by a new emotion.

He walked on the sidewalk so that, if eyes peered out at him, he could be seen to go to the corner and turn down the next street. Once there, he doubled back through the brush and came to the small rear door of the jail.

He kneeled beside it, and, drawing a little soft fold of chamois from his pocket, he spread it out and exposed its contents—a number of little flat shards of steel not much larger than needles. One of these he used to probe the lock of the door.

It was not satisfactory, and he changed to another probe with which he worked only a moment before he heard a light clicking sound inside the lock. The handle then gave to his touch, and he pushed the door slightly ajar.

Behind him, he heard the noise of deep voices gathering in a chorus, and the treading of feet that seemed as numerous as the march of an army out of step.

VI

He slipped through the door, closed it softly behind him. He found himself in a small room lighted by a single lamp that hung from the ceiling. Cells of steel bars were set against the four walls. Half a dozen of them were occupied. But he found the place of Reardon at once, in a corner. The big, quiet, shadowy figure spoke to him as clearly as words, and he went at once to the door of the cell.

"Hello," sang out a voice. "Who's the mug that comes in through the back door?"

Bristol turned and stretched out an arm.

"If you never saw a deputy sheriff before," he said, "I'll give you a close look, pretty soon. Maybe I'll show you the way the fist of a deputy feels, too."

"Never mind," said the other, pressing a round, red-bearded

face close to his bars. "I thought for a minute that something funny might be comin' along. But I recognize the breed by the lingo. You're the kind that couldn't drink soup without a nightstick, if you was in a town."

Bristol was working at the lock of the cell door. It gave to him almost instantly, and he walked inside.

Reardon had risen. He said: "Bristol, this is a brave thing and a grand thing for you to do, but I don't want it. I'm going to face this out. If I break jail, I'll be a criminal all the rest of my life."

"D'you want to stay here?" asked Bristol, already on his knees and working over the manacles that held the feet of the prisoner together and pinioned him to the wall. "Listen a minute and you'll hear the crowd coming down the street. They're coming to hang you, Tom."

He heard a whistling gasp above him. The tremor through the body of Reardon was so great that even his ankles quivered and made the little steel links of the chain chime softly against each other.

The bawling voice of the red-whiskered tramp across the way came suddenly through the room again.

"What kind of a deputy are you, unlockin' your man with a picklock? Who are you, brother?"

There was no answer from Bristol.

The tramp shouted: "If you take him, you take me, too! You take the whole of us, or else I'll shout for the sheriff. Answer me, buddy."

Desperately Bristol worked at the lock that secured the chains. It was unlike any he had tried before. He had spent his hours laboring with new devices, new inventions of the locksmiths. As a rule he could decipher them quickly enough, but this was a case when he found his skill gone, as it were.

Stubbornly the lock resisted the anxious, questioning touch of his probe.

"Hey!" yelled the voice of the tramp. "Hey, Sheriff! Hey, Dolan! Jail break! Jail break! Jail break!"

Bristol flinched. Fear worked like cold quicksilver through the middle of his back. Sweat was running under the pits of his arms. And still, out of the distance, he could hear the approaching murmur of the crowd.

An inner door slammed open.

"What's the damned nonsense in here?" asked the voice of Sheriff Dolan.

"Look yonder, you dummy!" cried the red-bearded tramp. "There . . . the Bristol cell!"

The sheriff was not wearing a sombrero but a small cap whose lightness he preferred when he was indoors, for to go with a completely uncovered head always gave him a sense of nakedness. Now this hat was jerked from his hair and tossed into the air. The boom of a gun and the crash of a .45-caliber slug against the wall, all in a moment, told the sheriff that things were going wrong.

He leaped back, more agile than a cat, through the door behind him. The door slammed loudly.

As the echoes of that slamming rang trembling through the room, Jack Bristol put away his revolver and called: "The next fellow who sings out, he gets the next slug, and not through the cap!"

There was silence through that room. There was hardly a breath drawn as Bristol kneeled to his work again.

He could hear excited voices in the corridor outside of the cell room. He heard the running of feet and the rumble of the crowd immediately at hand. Then there was a distinct noise of battering on the outer door of the jail.

In another moment they would be flooding in. For to the

sheriff these were friends in a time of need.

But excited hurry would do no good. It was the time for the deepest, the most unperturbed concentration. So Jack Bristol deliberately sat down cross-legged and vanished the world from his mind.

Above him, Tommy Reardon, shaking like a leaf in body and in voice, was groaning.

"It's too late. Save yourself, Bristol. We'll both be caught . . . the lynchers are here."

He might as well have spoken to a block of ice. Quietly, with half-closed eyes, Bristol was working with his bit of flat, stiff watch spring—and suddenly the lock gave, the shackles fell away.

Rising, he shoved a gun into the hand of Reardon.

"Don't use that unless you have to. If you have to . . . shoot low . . . shoot for the legs," he cautioned, and then leaped out through the open door of the cell.

There was no stir behind him.

He looked back and saw that Reardon, incredibly, had not moved. The gun hung from his limp hand. His face was so white that it seemed luminous, like phosphorescence. The gun he held made a dim, shuddering light.

Then Bristol understood.

The bravest of men can be crushed by the fear of the law, the fear of the crowd. Old criminals develop the terror acutely in a familiar form known as prison shakes, which overmaster them in moments of extreme danger. It was some such panic as this that now made it impossible for Reardon to stir hand or foot.

Disgust and horror made Bristol hesitate for the least part of a second. Should he try still to bring the coward away with him, or should he let the weakling take the fate that was coming?

And then it seemed to Bristol that the sea-green, calm eyes of the girl were looking in upon his mind again. He had told her, definitely, that he would bring Reardon away from trouble.

He ran back into the cell and gripped Reardon under the pit of the right arm.

"Move . . . run . . . lean on me. Start your legs going, and they'll work all the way," Bristol advised.

The door to the front of the jail dashed open again. Not one man, but many appeared, jamming through the aperture.

And there were guns—hosts of guns, as it seemed to Jack Bristol.

He fired at the floor. The smashed bullets would drive a shower of splinters before them.

He fired three times, making one long roll of thunder, the reports crowded one another so closely, and the heavy echoes boomed from the walls so continuously.

A frantic yelling broke from the men in the doorway. They disentangled themselves and scattered back. A fourth bullet hit the heavy door and slammed it shut behind them.

"Now!" ordered Bristol to Reardon, and he half led, half dragged him from the cell.

The red-whiskered tramp across the room was singing out: "Damn good, brother, whoever you are! Drop that yaller-livered hound and gimme a chance to ride with you. You got the cold nerve, old son. Lemme have a chance to work with you, and we'll crack the world like a nut!"

Bristol got Reardon to the rear door of the jail, and, with the open sky and the stars before him, strength came back to Tom Reardon for the moment, at least. He sprinted with all his might after his rescuer. They were at the verge of the brush before running men came around the rear corners of the jail and spotted the fleeing shadows.

The shouting rushed at them like a mighty wave, and Reardon instantly staggered in his stride. Terror made him limp again as they gained the place where the horses stood. And

Bristol had to use all his power to get the shambling bulk of his companion into the saddle. Bullets were clattering through the brush. Men came on the full charge, yelling. Then Bristol was able to get both horses started at last.

Through the brush, into the narrows of a lane they pressed the horses. They turned into an outer street of New Eden. Other riders were storming here and there behind them, blindly. And now they were beyond the town. The emptiness of the night received them, and the nightmare was shut away behind.

Right up the wavering trail they went, and from a distance they could hear the tumult still raging in New Eden, with occasional bursts of gunfire as the men of the town opened fire on shadows or fictions of the mind.

They were far into the region of safety before Bristol drew rein.

"Do you know a fellow called Cal Thompson, back there in New Eden?" he said.

"Bristol," said Reardon, "I'd rather be dead . . . than alive and know what I know about myself."

"What d'you know about yourself?"

"That I'm yellow."

"Nobody knows that until it's been proved."

"It was proved on me. I was too scared to move. I was stiff as ice. I'm a coward, Jack."

"All you needed was a chance to put your hands on them," said Bristol. "The minute that happened, you would have been yourself. And the main thing now is to stop mourning about it."

"Aye, I'll stop," agreed Reardon sadly. "Bristol, when you came back into that cell, you came back to get a dog. But . . . I'll stop talking about it."

"Good," said Bristol. "And now tell me about this fellow Cal Thompson and what he means to you."

"He's nothing to me. Fond of my girl. That's all."

"That all? You can write him down in red, Tommy. He was the fellow who almost put your head inside a noose, tonight. There's a lot more poison in him than there is in a snake."

Reardon made no answer. He rode on with his head fallen.

"Where are you heading?" asked Bristol.

"I don't know. I'll keep on till the horse stops. That's all."

For a long moment, Bristol considered. He had done a great deal, on this night, that would need a lot of explaining to his gang. He could see a way of serving Reardon and helping himself at the same time, now, so he said: "You come along with me. I'll put you up at the camp. You're going to be my Number One man until I find a way of shipping you out. Understand that? We'll work this game together until we see the best way out for you."

VII

When they got back to the camp, it was close to dawn. Accompanied by Reardon, Bristol rode down to his shack and then fired three shots in rapid succession into the air. At once nine or ten armed men came with a rush through the doors of the other two shacks. They were only half dressed, but they were ready for action, one and all.

Bristol said briefly: "I've been looking for a Number One man for a long time. Now I've got him. His name's Reardon, and he cost us forty thousand dollars and a little trouble, tonight. He's going to be worth it. And I'll tell you what . . . when he speaks, every man of you can jump. He'll represent me when I'm away."

Utter silence received this statement.

Then the voice of Sid Lester asked: "That mean that all the money you got from the bank of New Eden has gone into buying up this Reardon, or whatever he is?"

"That's what it means. Don't you like it?"

There was no answer, and, after a pause, Bristol took Reardon into the shack. He lit a lantern and pointed out the second bunk, and pulled down an extra roll of blankets. Then he saw the strained, pale face of Tom Reardon.

"I'll be a rotten lieutenant for you," said Reardon. "You didn't mean what you said, a minute ago."

"You're the best man I can find, anyway," answered Bristol with an assurance that he did not feel. "You're the brother of Kate Reardon, and that means that you can eat any two of these fellows for breakfast. Go to sleep. In the morning you'll have a new heart under your ribs."

But in the morning, in the gray of the dawn, word came to Jack Bristol that a certain youth who had been mixed up in a few shooting scrapes at last had come into the mountains in the hope of enlisting himself in Bristol's band. He was waiting at the mouth of the southern pass.

Business like this could not be postponed, and therefore Bristol left Reardon behind him and went straight up into the pass, at once. He found a big, blond-headed young fellow of nineteen waiting for him among the rocks. With a face of stone, Bristol listened to the other's story.

It took a good bit of time in the telling. For an hour, Bristol let the youth chat on. Then he began to draw conclusions.

"Partridge," he said, "you're sure that you'll never want to settle down and be a regular cowpuncher?"

"Me? Why should I? I hate the work," said Dick Partridge with conviction.

"You hate work because you're hardly grown up," answered Bristol. "You're still soft."

"Oh, I ain't so soft," said Dick Partridge, and he narrowed his eyes and fixed them firmly on the outlaw.

"Not with your fists . . . not with guns," answered Bristol. "But you're too soft to stand a winter riding the range, or a long roundup, or anything that makes a long strain on a man."

Partridge was silent.

Bristol went on: "You say you have a father and a mother and a brother and a pair of sisters."

"What have they got to do with it?" asked Partridge.

"Your family pays a lot more attention to your younger brother than they do to you. And you're jealous, Dick."

"The devil I am!" exclaimed Partridge. "Besides, I don't take this kind of talk from nobody, including you, Bristol."

"Good," said Bristol. "If you don't take this kind of talk from me, or from anybody else, go back home and show them that you're not a sulky young fool, always spoiling for a fight. Show 'em that you're a man. They'll make plenty of fuss over you, then."

"I'll never go back," declared Dick Partridge.

"What's the matter?" asked Bristol. "Does your kid brother lick you?"

"Him?" snorted Partridge. "He's weak as a girl. I could smash him with one hand."

"Because he's weak and sickly, the folks pay a lot of attention to him, and you're fool enough to be jealous, are you?" demanded Bristol.

"Who told you anything about being jealous?" shouted Partridge.

He was in a fighting fury, by this time, but Bristol merely smiled at him.

"Listen, Dick," he said, "you think that you're more welcome other places than you are in your home. You've stepped out and proved that you can shoot fast and straight. Now you're going to startle folks by coming into my gang. What sort of people do you think I have with me?"

"I know you've got a great outfit," said Dick Partridge with a tone of the greatest respect. "I wasn't trying to horn in as one of the regular men. I know you've got a picked outfit. And I don't mind being the roustabout. I'll saddle horses and run errands, till you think that I'm fit to go and ride the trail with the rest of the men. I wanna prove myself to you, and then see if you can't use me, chief."

"Let me tell you what those other fellows are," answered Bristol. "A lot of mangy dogs. Murderers. Crooks that I can't trust when my back's turned. I keep them because I can use them. That's all. Do you want to rub shoulders with dirt like that? They get nothing out of me except money. Is that what you want?"

The youth stared.

"Listen to me," said Bristol. "I don't know why I'm talking like this. I know your record. I could start using you right now. But in a month you'd be a drinking, sneaking, thieving rat like the rest of them. I'll tell you what. Go back home and stick out the year. If you still feel the same way about this . . . and I'm still alive . . . try to find me again, and I'll take you in. Now, you shake hands and go home."

Slowly Dick Partridge held out his hand.

"What beats me is where and how you found out about Joe," he declared. "I didn't talk much about him."

"There had to be a sore spot somewhere. I just tried a little guessing. Look here. Joe is the weakling, the sick boy. The women always fuss over that kind. But down in their hearts they want a fellow like you, that's sure to be a man."

"Aye, but I'll be back by the end of the year," said Dick Partridge. He jerked up his head. "I'm just going to show 'em," he said, "that I can do my job and grin and never show what I'm thinking. It's been wonderful to talk to you. I'll never forget . . . and you'll sure see me at the end of a year's time."

He went off, sitting very straight, turning twice to wave back to the outlaw, and Jack Bristol watched him out of view, with amazement. It was his own act that astonished him. Never in his life had he seen better material for a longrider than had appeared in that youth, but something had stopped him.

Was it because he had been learning something new, recently, retesting life, finding new values and meanings? Perhaps one essentially clean-minded fellow like Tommy Reardon was enough to have on hand. But he wanted with him, on the trail that runs outside the law, no fellows who had taken the wrong path simply because of excess of spirit or boyish adventurousness.

As he turned back down the mouth of the narrows, he began to wonder about his own beginning. What had driven him outside the law? Had there been confirmed villainy in his heart from the first? Or had he, like a foolish plant, taken root in the wrong soil?

At least he knew one thing. There had been no one to discourage him. No, the older men had looked on him partly in amusement and partly in admiration. He had felt that he was a hero, making himself the peer of older men.

The sun was well up when he rode down into his valley. He felt well. He felt extremely well. The thunder and the bright springing of the waterfall was like a special song composed and sung for him. He seemed to know what the music meant.

In the distance he could see a circle of his men gathered under the wide limbs of a tree to enjoy the first brilliance of the sun before it became too fiercely hot.

Who could deny that there was a careless joy in this life? Who could deny the exquisite wine of freedom? And had he not been wrong in shunting Dick Partridge away from this pleasure?

As he crossed the bottom of the valley, he saw one man leave the group and walk with bent head toward his own shack. He was surprised by that. They knew that they were forbidden to enter the place, and they had received a lesson on the subject recently.

But now it seemed to him that the outline, the height of the man, identified him as Tom Reardon. Bristol was almost sure, when the fellow walked straight in through the doorway and disappeared into the cabin.

As Bristol came up to the group under the tree, there was something odd in their attitude. Sid Lester was laughing, and staring at him.

"That's your forty-thousand-dollar beauty, is it?" asked Sid Lester. "Well, you been sold, chief. He's been and taken water right here and now."

"He . . . Tom Reardon took water?" demanded Bristol.

"Himself," answered Lester.

And there was a hum of bitter agreement from the rest of them.

"We *all* owned a slice of that money you throwed away on Reardon," said Lester, "and he ain't nothing but a yaller dog."

A chill that was not from the wind spread over the face and through the blood of Bristol.

"*I* called him," said Lester. "I told him he didn't look like forty thousand dollars' worth of anything. I told him he didn't look like forty cents, to me. And he took it. He *took* it. He hung his head and went off like a cur."

Sid Lester laughed loudly and rolled his eyes over the appreciative faces of his companions.

There was only one thing for Bristol to say, and he said it.

"The point is, Sid," he explained, "that I told Reardon to keep out of trouble while I was away. Except for that, he would have torn you in two."

"Yeah? He would, would he?" Lester sneered.

"You'll be seeing, later on," said Bristol, and went straight to the cabin.

When he entered, he saw Reardon stretched, face down, on a bunk, his hands, above his head, gripped hard in the folds of a blanket, his body twisted and shaken by a silent agony.

Bristol stood by him, looking quietly down.

Was it true, then? Had the whole heart and soul of Tom Reardon been shattered back there by the experience in the jail, with the frightful dread of lynching ever present before his eyes?

VIII

No problem like this had ever come into the mind of Bristol before. He had met and smashed many a strong man. That had been his joy and his profession. But this was an opposite task, and how could the soul and the spirit of a man be recreated?

He said briskly: "Sit up, Tom."

Reardon thrust himself up and swung his legs to the floor. His head was down. He looked like an exhausted man.

"I've taken . . . ," he began.

"Be quiet," answered Bristol. "I know what's happened. And I've put it right."

"You? You couldn't put it right," groaned Reardon, jerking up his head.

"I told them that you quit because you were told by me not to get into trouble while I was away."

"Did they believe that?"

"You're going back there and prove it . . . on Sid Lester. That's the big, burly hound that bullied you."

"You don't understand, Jack." Reardon sighed. "Something's gone out of me. There's no nerve left. I've been lying here wanting to cry like a baby."

"Sure you have," said Bristol. And he went on, lying smoothly: "I've been the same way myself."

"You?" cried Reardon, raising to his feet by sheer astonishment.

"It's being warmed up that makes the difference. You had a

shock . . . back there in the jail. And the blood seemed to run out of you, eh?"

"Yes," muttered Reardon.

"I've had the same thing happen. And what a man needs to do is to warm himself up, afterward. If you're down in a fight . . . fight again."

"I don't follow that," said Reardon. "But if you can teach me what you mean . . . if you can make me into a man again . . . I'll owe you more than my life."

"Ever box?" asked Bristol.

"Most of my life. But I couldn't put up my hands now. There's a weakness that's running through my arms. I can't get my breath. I feel sick. And it's fear, that's all. I'm a coward, Jack."

"Pull off your boots, and put a pair of these on your hands," said Bristol.

He took down boxing gloves from the wall and tossed a pair on the bunk. He drew off his own boots and stood in his stocking feet, fitting another pair of gloves on his hands. He knew what he had to do. The thing had come to him by inspiration the moment he heard that Reardon had boxed. If he had skill, together with his size and strength, he needed only heart in order to make himself formidable.

Those gloves had meant a great deal in Bristol's camps. When the blood ran high among his men, he was always willing to put on the gloves with any of them, and though there were always heavier, more powerful men than he among his followers, never once had any of them been able to master him. His uncanny speed of hand and foot was always too much for them.

"Stand up," said Bristol. "Now, I'm going to tell you this. I've licked every one of those fellows out there with the gloves. I've licked 'em more than once, too. And I'm going to lick you, Reardon, unless you put up a man's fight. But I'll tell you what will happen. After we've hit each other a few times, you'll find that your confidence will come back to you."

"Will it?" asked Reardon, staring with wide, agonized eyes of hope.

He stepped out and raised his gloves. Whatever panic was in him, training made him, automatically, raise a good, high guard.

Jack Bristol tried it, not with the flashing serpent-tongue left of which he was a master, but with a comparatively crude, roundhouse hook.

The blow was put aside. He tried again, much harder. He saw Reardon crouch and blink a little as the blow started, but instinct and long practice enabled him to block that punch, also. And a third time—now with all his might—Bristol smashed away with the identical blow.

Of course it was caught again, easily. A child could have done as much at a third repetition. And Reardon was standing a little straighter.

"You've got a good guard, there," said Bristol, shaking his head. "But take this!"

He slammed a long, straight, hard right at Reardon. If the punch had been aimed for the head, it would have knocked him flat. As it was, it shot through the air just past his cheek. And they clinched. There was a slight shudder in the body that closed against Bristol's.

"You ducked that well," he panted, and then he backed out of the clinch.

Reardon tried his first punch. It was a very half-hearted left—straight enough, but with a wincing uncertainty behind it. Bristol had almost to shift his head into its path to enable it to land, but land it did.

Again the left started. Again Bristol let it land, and this time there was a bit of sting behind it. A third time it came, and now with a whip crack that honestly knocked Bristol back on his heels.

"Hello!" gasped Bristol. "What you got on that left of yours?"

Reardon grinned. No shamefaced smile, now, but a look of honest interest and some pride. His head was higher. He stood more lightly on his feet. The leaden cowardice had been lifted somewhat from his heart.

Dancing cautiously, he followed his advantage.

Bristol feinted twice at the head—he could have driven either punch home—and then brought up a mild right into the ribs of Reardon. He hit high, where the spring of the ribs is the greatest and the strongest. The kick of a mule would hardly have hurt a man in that special spot of the body.

"Sorry I let that one go. Did it hurt you?" asked Bristol, stepping back.

"Not a bit. Didn't feel it." Reardon chuckled.

"What are you made of, then? Iron?" asked Bristol.

Reardon came in with a good long left. It could have been ducked, but Bristol let it thud against his forehead, knocking him for the second time back on his heels.

A shadow swooped at him. He could have blocked that right cross easily. Instead, he let it come. A good, clean, thwacking blow, it cracked along his jaw. There was weight enough in the punch to make him sway to the side, and he let himself go, falling on his hands.

He lay there with his head down, forcing out great gasps.

Reardon was instantly on his knees beside the outlaw.

"I'm sorry, Jack," he said. "I forgot how much bigger I am than you. I shouldn't have let that one go. I didn't think it was so hard. It must have just clicked you on the button."

Bristol sat up, holding his head in both hands.

"Button?" he growled. "It would have broken the head of a steer, that one. Why didn't you tell me that you were a professional? Ever fought in the ring?"

"No," said Reardon. "Used to spar around a lot with one of the boys who was an old lightweight. That's all."

"You're a wonder," declared Bristol. "That left is a natural beauty, but the right is a devil. The top's still off my head."

He stood up, pulling against the hand of Reardon to lift himself. Again on his feet, he balanced uncertainly.

"*Whew!*" breathed Bristol, pulling off the gloves. "I've had enough of that." He hung both pairs of gloves on the wall again. Then he patted the shoulder of Reardon. "I can feel the muscle here," he said. "And that's where the damage comes from. That's what crumples the other fellow. You've got a wad of India rubber out here on the point of your shoulder. No, sir, I don't want to take you on with the gloves again."

"D'you mean it, Jack?" asked Reardon happily.

"Mean it? Of course I mean it. What about the nerves you were talking of?"

"Why, I feel a lot better," said Reardon.

"Of course you do," said Bristol. "I knew you would. How about going out there and stepping into Sid Lester, now?"

"Not . . . ," began Reardon.

But Bristol was already at the door of the shack, calling: "I've told Reardon he can go after you, Sid! Pull yourself together and try to take it like a man, will you?"

The announcement startled the entire group. Sid Lester gaped as though he had been already hit.

"Wait a minute, Jack," said the pale-faced Reardon as Bristol turned around. "I don't think. . . ."

Bristol pretended not to hear. Instead, he doubled himself up with pretended laughter. Slapping his hands together, he said: "Pull on your boots, Tom. Go out there now and slaughter him. Don't kill him, though. Keep his head bobbing on the end of that long left for a few minutes so that I'll be able to have my fun. And when you use that right of yours, it'll ring a bell every time."

He was pushing Reardon toward the door, slapping him on the back. And so, rather weak-kneed, Reardon stepped out into the open. Bristol walked beside him, jauntily laughing, toward the spot where Lester was pulling off his coat and rolling up his sleeves. It was the cheerful laughter of Bristol that wiped the sneer from the face of Lester.

But he had the fighting heart of a brute beast, after all, and his hands were hardly up before he was charging.

Eagerly, with a heart that swelled against a mighty tension, Jack Bristol watched Reardon flinch, then at the last minute flick out with the long left.

It should have missed, if Lester had possessed one ounce of skill in addition to his strength. As it was, Lester simply rammed his face against that stiffened left arm as against a wall.

The shock brought him up standing, rocking back a little. He was wide open, his guard down a bit, and anyone who had ever worn boxing gloves could not fail to see that vast opportunity.

On the pale face of Reardon appeared a faint flash of ferocity. He stepped in, rising on his toes, and, as his heels fell, he struck with all his might.

It was a very pretty right hook that curved across the wide shoulders of Sid Lester. Right beside the point of the jaw, with a sound like the spatting of palms together, that punch went home.

Big Sid Lester went down in sections, so to speak. His arms dropped first. His knees sagged. His head fell forward on his chest. He would have spilled weakly to the ground, unconscious, but Reardon himself caught the inert hulk and lowered it gently.

"A real pug," murmured someone.

IX

There should have been a ripple, at least, of applause. For these were fellows who admired strength of hand and a hard fist, and not one of them possessed the swift, sure eye that had enabled Bristol to see how much luck and the stupidity of Sid Lester had given victory into the hands of Reardon. Even so, that final right cross had been beautifully conceived and beautifully executed.

But the men of the gang stood about in a grim silence after the one remark. That silence was a weight on Bristol's mind, as he went back with Reardon to his shack.

Inside the little house, Reardon was walking on air.

"You knew, Jack," he said. "It was a sort of a disease. And now the germ's dead in me. I'm healed again. It was as though all the blood were running out of me through an open wound. Fear. There's nothing in the world as sickening as that." He threw a clenched fist high above his head. "I'm my own master now!" he cried. "And you've done it for me, Jack. The first time I blocked a punch of yours, I felt like a different man. But . . . what's the matter? Is there something wrong?"

The cold, set expression of his friend had stopped him.

"The lads are feeling their oats a little," said Bristol. "They're looking at me in a queer way, Tom. And I'll be hearing from them before long. Let's cook up a meal."

They rattled the stove to life and built a rousing fire. The chief cook was Bristol. The assistant was Reardon, and, as he worked, he broke continually into song.

The coffee was simmering in the big, black pot, when a hand rapped at the door, and Reardon saw a tall man with a tanned, cadaverous face standing near the threshold. He wore a pair of Chinese mustaches—frail, drooping tufts of blond hair that wavered from the corners of his mouth when he talked.

"Could I have a word with you, chief?" he asked.

"Blaze away, Tankerton," answered Bristol. "Come in."

"I ain't gonna be favored above the rest of the boys," answered Tankerton. "The rest of them can't come in, and I ain't gonna come inside."

"That's a start," said the chief. "What d'you want?"

He walked closer to the door and looked down into the face of Tankerton. He had a habit of staring right into the eyes of his men, and they could endure it no more than could wild beasts. But as he looked at Tankerton, now, the big fellow regarded him, in return, with a steady, ugly look.

"It ain't what I want," said Tankerton. "It's what the boys want. It's about *him!*"

Bristol stepped suddenly through the door and confronted his man. He was not anxious that this dialogue should come to the ears of Tom Reardon.

"Go on," invited Bristol.

"It ain't easy to go on," said Tankerton. "I got my share of nerve, I think, but it ain't easy to talk to you. You're a hard man, Bristol."

"Leave that out," said Bristol.

"We pulled straws, and I got the short one," said Tankerton. "That's why I'm here."

"Damn your reasons for being here," said Bristol. "What have you to say? The coffee's getting cold, in there."

Tankerton's jaw thrust out. He said, through barely moving lips: "It's the kid, there. We been working for you for years, some of us, and we've never had the kind of treatment that he's got."

"You've had what you deserved," said Bristol.

"How come?" asked Tankerton. "That's what we want to know. All we want to know is why he's so great. He's got a good stance and he's got a good right hook. I seen it land. But what's he got outside of that?"

"Why should I explain what he's got?" asked Bristol.

"I ain't fool enough to press you," said Tankerton. "But the boys look at it like this. All they know about Reardon is that he tries to stick up a stage and like a fool tries to do it with an empty gun. And then he's caught and nabbed and slung into the jail. And out of that jail he would've been taken and lynched by the mob in your name, if you hadn't showed up and paid down forty thousand cash, and then broke open the jail to get at him.

"Then you bring him out here and put him up in your own shack, and you kick the rest of us in the face if we come near your quarters. We wanna know what the meaning is."

"Because it pleases me to act that way," said Bristol. "Is that answer enough for you?"

Tankerton scowled darkly. "We figger that we got forty thousand dollars' worth of reasons for asking that question," he said.

"You don't like the price I've paid for him in cash? Well, the gang may get an extra cut on the next job we do."

"Them of us that live through it."

"I don't like the way you put that, Tankerton."

"The boys don't like the way you're dealing to them just now," answered Tankerton. "And I don't blame them a whole lot."

"Ah, you don't blame them? That's because your brain isn't working as well as it ought to." A heavy Colt winked into his hand.

Tankerton, with a gasp, jerked out his own weapon, but the revolver of his chief already had spoken, and the big sombrero, lifting from the head of Tankerton, spun away through the air.

"Keep your hat off, and your brain will be cooler," advised Bristol.

Tankerton turned, ran his hand over his naked head, and

then gave his chief a final glance across his shoulder. There was no good fellowship in this last look.

Beyond him, Bristol saw eight more of his men under the tree, all of them looking braced, as though ready to run forward. As though ready to run straight toward Bristol himself.

The chief went back into the shack. Steam and smoke rose in billows and clouds toward the ceiling, and at this moment, with wonderful dexterity, Reardon was flipping a flock of four pancakes into the air and catching them all in one sweeping gesture without permitting the batter to spatter out upon the floor. He settled the griddle back on the fire and struck a louder and a higher note in his song.

They had finished their breakfast before either spoke. Reardon said: "Chief, what are the plans?"

"I'm making them now, in my head," said Bristol.

"What sort of plans?"

"Travel."

"That's good. I travel with you?"

"You do."

"Where do we go?"

"Away."

"Yes. But where?"

"Anywhere so long as it's away from this outfit. They're on the rise, old son." He smiled mirthlessly at Reardon. "The boys out there are all ready to cook. And I can't give them a fire hot enough to do."

"You mean that they're getting out of hand?" asked Reardon.

"They're not getting out of hand. They're clear out already. Go collect your horse and get my gray along with it, will you?"

"You mean that we're to start now?"

"Pretty *pronto.*"

Reardon stood up with a start. He stood a little too straight, too stiff. The color of his face was not good.

121

"It's going to be a gunfight, chief?" he asked.

"What of that?" countered Bristol.

"Nothing," said Reardon. "I've . . . I've been picked out of the scum by you. I . . . I ought to be glad to have a chance to fight and die like a white man. I *am* glad. I'll be still gladder when the guns start."

Bristol regarded him with a steady eye.

"All right," he said. "Go get the horses like a good fellow, will you? I've got something to do here."

Big Tom Reardon went out of the shack at once, with a pair of ropes. His chief set about an investigation of several packs that hung against the wall. He cut them open, and was spilling out the contents in order to pick out what he might want, when a long shadow bobbed across the threshold of the shack.

He thought it might be Reardon, already returned with the horses. Instead, he was amazed to see Kate Reardon on a mustang with the eyes of a deer.

She dismounted and stood in his doorway.

"Hello, Jack!" she called to him. "Are you shaking hands with me this morning?"

"I am," said Bristol.

She caught his hand with both of hers and gripped it hard. "Everything that a Reardon can give you . . . now . . . always . . . to the end of the world!" cried the girl. "I've been through New Eden. I've talked to the men in the streets. And every man of them agrees that it was the finest, coolest, most devilish bit of work that ever was done. I listened . . . and it was like drinking fine spring water when you're thirsty. It was the most beautiful thing that I ever heard. It was the very best. There's no man in the world worthy of being mentioned with you, Jack."

He had thought that she was very cool and calm, the other day. But this was different. Her voice did not burst up into the shrill soprano of most girls, even now. But her eyes had a warmth that took hold of him. There was space and strength in her soul to grasp a great emotion and keep it.

He smiled at her for one moment as he never had smiled at another human being. He felt as though he were shouting things aloud to her, revealing his soul, as he smiled.

And they were drawn close, wonderfully close.

Yet what he said was simply: "How did you get through into the valley?"

"Why, I just came through," she answered.

"Was Butch up there, or someone who recognized you?"

"I didn't see a soul."

"You didn't. . . . Wait a moment, you mean that you didn't see a single man in the pass?"

"No. Should I have?"

He drew back from her a little.

"I knew that trouble was coming," he said, "but I didn't think it would come as fast or as big as this."

X

He went to the door of the shack. There was no sound or sight of a human being in the valley except Reardon bringing in the two horses on the run, and waving his hat as he came. That would be because he had recognized his sister's horse.

There was no one to be seen, but no doubt some of his men were inside either of the two shacks.

He called out sharply: "Hey, waddies!"

There was no answer. The wind out of the northwest whistled, thin and small, beside his ear, as though in mockery. And he heard the beating of the waterfall like the noise of trampling hoofs in retreat.

Something had gone very wrong. There was a standing order to his men that they should be within his call, never less than six men ready to spring to arms. That had been his system. And now not a soul was near enough to respond to his command.

Bristol's eyes were dim and distant with thought as he turned and watched the affectionate greeting between the girl and her brother.

"*You* did it," Reardon was insisting. "Nobody but you would have thought of coming up here and trying to get Jack Bristol on the job. Nobody but you would have been *able* to find him or persuade him. But look. . . ."

"Hush," said the girl. "There's something wrong. There's something in the air. What is it, Jack?"

"Twelve gunmen are in the air, in the clouds . . . and thunder and lightning is likely to start at any minute," answered Bristol.

They both watched him, quietly, with the sort of assurance that men give to old and famous leaders. Whatever he decided, that would be the right thing to them.

He watched them with a singular intensity, in turn. He had had plenty of brave people put their trust in him, in the past, but they had been crooks, without exception. This was another matter.

He said quietly: "I think that they've had enough of me. I'm sure that they mean mischief, now. They've all worked for me, but it's always been under the lash. They're tired of the whip, I suppose."

"What do you think they'll do?" asked the girl. "Simply ride off and leave you?"

"Fellows like that don't simply ride off and leave," answered the chief. "If they've made up their minds to chuck me, they'll try to take my skin off, first. They're off somewhere putting their heads together, just now. They're busily deciding how to push through a campaign against me. They even took the guards out of the passes. Well, while they're deciding, the three of us may be able to slip through and get out of their hands. We'll start now . . . and we'll ride hard."

They were in the saddle instantly and rushing their horses toward the western end of the valley, where the waterfall sprang from the high edge of the cliff, and where the trail went up toward the southern pass. They left the easily sloping floor of the valley. They gained the top of the first hill and found themselves in the narrows of the pass, winding in and out among the big, jagged rocks.

It was hot in the pass. The wind was shut away. The heat waves rose trembling and shimmering above the blazing stones, and the horses toiled like slaves in a pit, with the sweat starting out in a thousand little bright lines down the neck and the shoulders.

"Two minutes more, and we'll be in the clear," said Bristol.

"And then where?" asked the girl.

"Over the hills and far away," said Bristol, smiling a little.

"Alone, or Tom with you?" she asked again.

"Tom," said Bristol, "there's a lot of nervousness in you. You might not like the sort of a life I'm going to lead."

"What sort?" asked Reardon.

"I'm going to travel a thousand miles from here, and, still inside the Rockies, I know a valley where I can drop out of sight like a stone into the sea. Or like a buzzard into the sky," he added. He chuckled. "I'm going to stay there and build a herd of my own."

"You?" cried Reardon. "You mean that you're really going to settle down? What's changed you?"

Bristol looked at the girl, steadily, shamelessly.

And she, taking his glance casually at first, began to lift her head, at last, while a deep color spread over her face.

"Is that it?" asked Reardon curiously, as he glanced from one of them to the other. "Why, you two don't know one another at all."

"Knowing isn't a matter of years," said the girl. She kept watching Bristol carefully, as though there were a lesson in his face that had to be learned.

In fact, he was changed, and still changing. The tightness had passed away from his mouth; the sharp light had left his eyes; he looked younger, and he was casting off time with every moment that passed.

"I thought the free life was the real life," said Bristol. "But down there in the jail I was ready to run, Tom. I was ready to skin out and save my own hide, and then I remembered. You know, Kate. You know what I remembered."

"A promise?" she asked.

"That's it. And I've been thinking ever since. Nobody's really free. A rope holds a good horse . . . a promise holds the right sort of a man. And this life I'm leaving . . . I'll never turn back to it. Summer can't burn me into it, and winter can't freeze me back into the old ways."

With a sort of glory coming into his voice, he was saying this when his head was struck forward by a blow.

Big Tom Reardon, reaching quickly with both arms, caught the body as it spilled out of the saddle. Looking down at the loosely fallen head, he saw the crimson streak of blood that welled out through the hair at the back of the skull.

Afterward, the report of the rifle clanged against their ears, traveling faintly through the thin mountain air.

It was the girl who looked up and saw the figure of a man on the edge of the cliff to their right, far above. She saw him now brandishing his rifle high above his head, and dancing with arms and legs against the sky.

This was the answer of the gang to its leader, and one bullet seemed to have been enough.

Kate, dismounting under the lee of some great rocks, helped to receive the weight of the limp body. It was too much for her, rolling in her arms and sliding down to the ground.

Big Tom Reardon was beside her instantly. He picked up Bristol like a loose sack and carried him quickly inside a nest of big rocks that rose almost like the ruins of Cyclopean walls. There were plenty of gaps in those walls, but they offered some shelter, at least.

"They've killed him," Reardon whispered. "Kate, they've murdered him."

She was the color of pale stone, but she was as steady as a stone, also. Leaning over the prostrate figure, she saw that the eyes were partially open. There was a sickening, meaningless smile on the lips.

When she pressed her ear against his breast, she felt the warmth still in his body, but she was sure that that warmth was a liar. For she could make out no heartbeat whatever.

Men said that there was only one sure way—to see whether or not a mirror was misted by the breath of a senseless being. But she had no mirror.

"Yes," she said, "he's dead. He's dead. . . . No, Tommy. D'you see? There's still blood coming from that wound behind the head. Blood doesn't run from a dead body, does it?"

"I don't know," answered the agonized voice of Reardon.

Up the ravine the clattering of the hoofs of horses began— horses ridden at headlong speed down the rocky slope of the pass. And then the voice of a yelling chorus broke on the ears of Reardon.

"There's a spot of whiskey in this," said Reardon, pulling out a flask. "Let me hold his head. . . ."

"That stuff will only choke him," said the girl. "Give me the water . . . that's much safer. Give me the canteen."

He reached it for her instantly.

"If he's got a fighting chance, give it to him, Tommy!" she cried up at him. "Stop them before they close in on us. Hold them. You've got to hold them back."

Reardon, springing to his feet, was already whipping the length of a shining Winchester out of the saddle scabbard of Duster. Now he stood at a gap in the rocks, the rifle at the ready.

But the rocks higher up the ravine obscured his vision. And the yelling of the gang came like a fatal music into his mind.

It was no use. When he saw them, they would be already close on the little natural fortress. There was only one hope for him—and that was to scutter away on foot, sneaking from rock to rock. They would not mind him, if they had their chief's body to gloat over—the life of their chief to finish, perhaps.

That was how sickening fear ran through the soul of Tom Reardon.

What was it that Bristol had said? That all men feel great fear until the first blow is struck, the first blood drawn. But there would be no chance, here, for first blows. The first blow would be the last one.

He looked back into that scene in the shack, down there in the valley. And, as he remembered, a cold smile twisted his face. It had seemed perfectly real and true, at the time, but now he could see that the whole affair had been a sham, carefully organized by Bristol to restore courage to his friend. The clumsiness with which that fellow of steel and lightning had struck out; the brittle manner in which the outlaw had apparently gone to pieces at the first real blow that struck him; no, the whole thing had been a sham planned and put through by Bristol to restore the heart of his companion.

But where was Bristol, now, to restore courage to the soul of any man?

Pain suddenly slashed the shoulders of big Tom Reardon. Across his back, like a knife cut, his flesh was ripped. And afterward he heard the ringing report of the rifle on the cliff.

That murderer up yonder—he was at his work again. A second later he might drive a better-aimed bullet right through the heart of Reardon.

But Reardon did not wince from his post. He did not flee. For with the pain there rushed through him an immense glory of hot courage and conviction.

His own life did not matter, if he could break the charge of those yelling fiends who came whooping down the valley.

So he stood his ground, with leveled, ready rifle.

XI

Out around the edges of the upper rocks poured the throng. He met them with bullets. A big man with a red face—raw-red, spotted with freckles—that fellow rode with the racing group of the left, shouting like a giant.

Reardon shot for the body of Butch but struck the mustang through the head, instead. The poor little horse dived into the ground while Butch was flung into the air. Head down, his body clapped against the flat face of a rock, then slumped and lay in a broken heap. Butch would never ride or yell for blood again.

His companions in that section of the riders had switched their mounts away to the side, disappearing among the boulders.

But there on the right were no fewer than five men, racing their ponies.

At Tankerton, Reardon took a snap shot.

The head of the big fellow flipped over on his shoulder. Slowly his body inclined to the side. He looked almost like a headless horseman for an instant, then he spilled out of the saddle, swinging sidewise toward the ground.

Such deadly marksmanship was too hard for even the nerves of the Bristol gang to endure. They were checking their horses; they were yelling with fear and scrambling away for shelter here and there among the rocks.

Reardon saw that much. Then a big-caliber rifle bullet smote the boulder beside his head and drove rock splinters into his cheek. That was no matter. The stinging of a dozen hornets— what was that to Reardon?

He knew, as he whirled, that he would have a chance for only a quick shot. He estimated the distance carefully, but like lightning. About two hundred yards, and at a distance above his head—the whole calculation was run through swiftly, briefly, and, as he turned, he instantly had the rifle in the correct position.

A bullet, at the same time, clipped through his right thigh. Yonder he saw the rifleman on the cliff, a black spot against the sky. He fired. At that distance and angle, who could tell what the result would be?

He saw the stranger rise and stand straight. He had missed, then? If so, he was dead—none of them could possibly escape.

But what was that gleaming thing that fell out of the hand of the man on the cliff? Could it be a rifle that he had dropped? And was he not leaning out at a strange angle over the edge of the cliff? He was—and now toppling forward, now clear of the edge of the rock, now falling in a slow spin through the air. He entered the shadow. Distinctly Reardon heard the shock of body as it struck the rocks beneath, unseen.

"Three," said Reardon. "There's three of 'em gone, Kate. And no matter what happens, I've paid my way, I guess."

She did not look up at him. She was crouched close to the body of Bristol, and it seemed to Reardon that she was trying to drive the strength of her own life, the breath of her own being, into the body of Jack Bristol.

Under his eyes the miracle was accomplished. For the bandaged head—how quickly she had made the wrapping—now turned a little, and a faint groan came from Bristol's lips.

A shout of joy broke from Reardon. He tried to make a step forward, but his right leg collapsed under him. He braced himself up on his hands, and saw Bristol suddenly sit up with a shake of the head.

"You've done it, Kate!" cried Reardon. "You've brought him back. Jack, listen to me. We've put a dent in them. Now that you're up, we'll smash right through them."

"You're hit," murmured Jack Bristol, and he stared at the blood-streaming body of his friend.

"Scratches," said Reardon. "You were right. You're always right. The first bit of blood, and I was easy again. It made me feel good . . . it took the shake out of my hands . . . and three of 'em are down and never will stand up again, Jack. Three of 'em. Tell me . . . are we paying our way?"

Bristol stood up. He was only a trifle unsteady on his legs. His eye was clearing constantly.

"It was only a graze of the skull," he declared. "I know by the ache of it. I've had it before. Kate, there's a job for us to do on poor Tom. Tom, you've saved the scalps of all of us." He looked down in wonder at the sprawling body of Tommy Reardon.

And Reardon laughed cheerfully back at him. "It's better to die white than to live yellow," he declared.

They gave him no answer to that. But the girl and Bristol exchanged one blazing, all-penetrating glance, filled with understanding. Tom Reardon had reached man's estate and he would never leave it.

They fell to work, rapidly, skillfully on the dressing of Reardon's wounds.

Out from the rocks, not far from them, a voice called: "Hello! Hello, Reardon!"

"Hi!" yelled Reardon in answer.

"We got Bristol dead as hell," answered the other. "You, Reardon, we're gonna deal with later on. But we'll give the girl a chance to get away. There's nine of us to scatter around through the pass, and you'll never get through. You hear us? We'll let the gal go. Let her step out now."

"I won't go," answered Kate Reardon. When she spoke, she raised her voice: "I'll stay here!"

"Mind you," shouted the other, "if you stay there, what's gonna happen to you when we rush that place after dark is more than I'll answer for."

"It's Sid Lester," said Bristol. "Let me speak to him."

He called cheerfully: "Hello, Sid!"

A shout of astonishment answered him.

"It was only a little graze of the skull, not a bullet through the brain the way the lad on the cliff told you," said Bristol. "Send up another good shot to the high rocks. I'd like to play the game all over with him. And the rest of you . . . if you want to rush this place, remember that I'll be glad to see you. Any of you!"

He heard distinctly an outbreak of curses, and groans of rage and disappointment.

Then silence settled over the narrow defile.

"What will they do?" asked Tom Reardon.

"They'll think for a while," replied Bristol. "They'll remember finally that there are only nine of them." Some of the cold disdain hardened about his mouth again as he mentioned the number. "Nine house dogs," he added, "ready to yell and to run."

"They won't give up," declared the girl. "They're too savage for that. They'll wait for the night and then try to steal up on us."

"Of course they will," said Bristol. "They'll wait for night, and then they'll try."

The heat was terrible. As for the water, it was conserved for

Tom Reardon, who had bled a good deal. A fever glazed his eyes before the afternoon was half ended, and by the evening his teeth were shuddering together in a chill, now and again.

Bristol took off part of his clothes and put them on his friend. Then he spent time cutting thick saddle blankets into strips that he bound carefully around the feet of the horses.

There were two ropes. He used them to sling a seat between the tall gray, Duster, and the girl's gentle mustang. And so the dimness of the twilight turned into dark night.

The stars were burning down closer through the heavens when Bristol said: "Now we start . . . up the pass."

"Up? Into the narrows? Why into the neck of the bottle, chief?" asked Reardon.

"Because they'll be expecting a retreat," said the girl. "They'll be down the pass, most of them. Only one or two to watch the narrows. Is that it, Jack?"

"That's it," he said. "I'm going ahead. You lead the horses, Kate. It isn't speed that'll turn the trick for us. It's only soft going . . . and a prayer, I suppose."

He gripped the hand of Tom Reardon. He leaned above Kate, silently, and kissed her. Then he left the big nest of boulders and went up the narrows, dissolving instantly among the shadows.

He went a hundred feet. Behind him, things stirred and whispered. The horses were making those sounds as they trudged along, led by the girl and carrying Tom Reardon slung between them.

A big, shadowy rock, before the eyes of Bristol, seemed to divide into two parts.

The smaller portion said: "That you, Charlie?"

"Aye," said Bristol. He took two more steps forward.

"Two are better'n one, where the chief's likely to show up," said the outlaw.

Bristol sprang and struck out through the darkness with his revolver.

The fellow dropped and lay in a heap.

Bristol pushed back the head and made out, even by starlight, the long face of Sid Lester. He poised the heavy gun for a second stroke, but could not give it.

He waited for the hushed escort to come up with him, and called softly back: "We're through the last guard. Go slow . . . go slow."

They went slowly, slowly. They reached the end of the narrows and turned up an untrailed mountainside. The wilderness before them had as many unexplored heights and valleys as the waves of the sea.

Once, from far behind, they thought that they heard shouting voices. And once they certainly made out the distant clangor of hoofs over rocks in an echoing ravine. But these noises dissolved, and they were still safe.

Long hours they struggled into the trackless ravines of the mountains until at last the dawn began to shine faintly from the east, making the mountains black.

The morning grew. From a highland, they saw beneath them the green glimmering of a beautiful valley with a silver streak of water through the midst of it.

There they halted.

Tom Reardon, with extreme weariness, closed his eyes to the pleasant prospect before them.

The other two stood close together on the rising ground. They neither touched nor spoke to one another, but their eyes were plunging deeper and deeper into the fathomless beauty of the morning and of the fair life that lay ahead, their pursuers having been eluded.

$\star$ $\star$ $\star$ $\star$ $\star$

GUNFIGHTERS IN HELL

$\star$ $\star$ $\star$ $\star$ $\star$

"Gunfighters in Hell" was Frederick Faust's final contribution to Popular Publication's *Star Western*. It was published under his Max Brand byline in the April 1935 issue. It is a tale of greed and romance, with a dramatic conclusion played out in the desert, a setting not often used by Faust, but one that he would use to perfection a year later in one of his most well-known stories, "Wine in the Desert" (6/7/36), published in *This Week*, the Sunday supplement of Hearst papers. This is the first time "Gunfighters in Hell" has appeared since its original publication.

I

Just off the rough double-rutted mountain trail, in the shadow of a group of huge granite boulders, a masked man waited, listening. From time to time his hand crept near the half-breed holster sagging at his hip, where rested an ivory-handled .45. His eyes, peering out from the slits in the black mask, were expectant, dancing, and yet there was a bitterness and a hardness in them, too, something that seemed to match the rock-like squarely built jaw and the cleft in his chin.

His thin lips compressed. Surely there was no chance for a mistake. He'd seen the buckboard miles back, glimpsed at a distance through the sage and the undergrowth of the bench land, and had raced his horse to this hidden place. But thus far there came no sign of it—neither wheel creak nor rapid-fire drumming of ponies' hoofs. He drew his gun, squinted at the cold blue metal, lifted the hammer part way, and twirled the cylinder.

Yes, it would pay him to wait . . . pay him well.

Meanwhile, far below him, the tongue of the buckboard kept jerking from side to side, the front wheels proceeding by lurches and pauses over the rutted, rocky trail. Other horses would have been maddened by the rattling, jerking, tossing wagon pole, but these two buckskin mustangs at a dog-trot would endure anything in the world. Their driver, Jimmy Harrigan, had taken them over worse places, and with a heavier load.

As for Jimmy himself, he felt this was the trail to heaven

because he had over $10,000 in his money belt and on the seat beside him was the girl he intended to marry. Mary Dickinson now supplied the first bumps on his trail to Paradise.

"Was I the way you expected to find me, Jimmy?" she asked, after she looked back toward her pony, which trotted to the side of the trail in order to escape the dust, almost chafing the lead rope against the spinning rim of the rear wheel.

"Why, just about," said Jimmy Harrigan. His name was more Irish than his blood, but he had the Irish fighting jaw, together with an eye almost too blue and gentle. "You were maybe a shade distant," he admitted. "But that doesn't matter. You rode all the way over to the crossing, and that shows that you still belong to me."

"Jimmy, I've changed."

"Well, I'm patient. I'll get used to a new Mary, if I have to."

"That's the way you've always won," she remarked. "Patience. When I said I'd marry you a year ago, you left the next day to make some money. You prospected for eleven months and lived on sagebrush and air, and then you strike it pretty big, sell out for ten thousand, and come back. You're ready to take up the old life where you left it. But suppose you can't?"

Harrigan smiled at her with perfect trust. "I can't?" he questioned softly.

"Life isn't a dead beef that stays put . . . it's a wild maverick," said the girl. "It kicks loose and goes on its own."

"Suppose so," he agreed mildly.

"Well, suppose all your patience isn't fast enough or strong enough to catch up with that maverick? Look, Jimmy, what's the difference between what I was when you left me and what I am now?"

"You're a year older,"

"I was nineteen. Now I'm twenty. I was a girl, and now I'm a woman. Jimmy, I rode all the way over to the crossing because I wanted to talk things out with you. I'm not sure I want to marry you, now."

"Ah, don't you?" said Harrigan. He slapped the off horse with the rein and added: "I'm sorry about that."

"And you, too," said the girl. "You've probably changed. If you'll open your eyes and take a second look, you may not want me now."

"No," said Harrigan. "Once I've made up my mind I never change it."

"How old are you?"

"Twenty-four."

"Then you're only a youngster. You don't know how much you'll change."

"I wanted you a year ago. I'll want you till I die," he said quietly.

She was silent for a moment, looking askance at him. "What do you intend to do? I mean with the future?"

He waved his hand. "This looks pretty good to me."

"You mean the cactus and the rocks and the mountains? Is that what looks pretty good to you?"

"I mean, it's the right size of things. Not much water, but it can be dammed up in tanks. Not much grass, but what there is of it is the finest cattle feed in the world. The land is cheap. I know the game. I've got ten thousand dollars to make my start with. And I've got a pair of hands that will never stop working. I guess I could live . . . partly . . . on the blue of the sky out here."

"But suppose you should change, Jimmy?" she cried. "Suppose that after a while you began to find it a lonely life, and suppose that you wanted to go to the city and live in a different way?"

"I'll never change," he said. "I'll never want anything else."

"But suppose *I* want something else?" she demanded.

"I'll have to be patient, then, and give you all that I can."

"Patience!" cried Mary Dickinson. And there was a queer mixture of disgust and admiration in her voice.

He said nothing, but he knew that some of the wild Dickinson blood was working in her. Steve Dickinson, her father, had led a wild life even for a wild country, and some of the tales of his doings were apt to throw a chill into the blood. And the girl, as she grew older, showed more and more the beauty of her dead mother and the high, proud head of her father.

Harrigan was still thinking of this when he drove the buckboard into a narrow way that was framed by great rocks on either side.

From the shadow of one of those rocks, a masked rider on a magnificent black horse appeared. The mask lay over the eyes and the bridge of the nose, only, and Harrigan thought he would never forget the exact look of the square chin, with the cleft in the center of it. The rider carried a revolver, held straight on Harrigan's chest.

"Stick 'em up, feller," he commanded. "Sorry, Miss Dickinson, but Harrigan is carrying a lot more money than he needs. Grab air, Harrigan."

Harrigan said nothing. The mustangs had stopped. Now the driver stood up and held his hands high above his head, obediently. The robber, riding close, used only his left hand to unfasten and take from Harrigan the heavy money belt.

"That's about all," said the bandit. "A dummy like you wouldn't have the sense to scatter his loot around. I guess I've got all you own. So long, Harrigan. Sorry, Miss Dickinson." And he reined his horse away among the rocks.

The cheerful clicking of hoofs at full gallop drifted back to the ears of Harrigan as he lowered his arms. Then he saw that Mary Dickinson was already out of the buckboard and mounting her horse.

"It's a year's work gone," said Harrigan calmly.

"But you've got patience!" cried the girl, reining her mustang beside the buckboard. "You haven't the nerve of a *man* to fight for your own, but you have the patience to go out and build up another stake . . . and have *that* taken away from you. I knew there was something like this wrong with you. I hope I never lay eyes again on the face of such a coward!"

She was gone before he could speak a word in answer.

It was not merely the year's work and the luck of a lifetime that the outlaw had taken from him.

Harrigan looked calmly around at the blue face of the sky, washed pale by the endless floods of sunlight. It was all changed for him.

Was he a coward? He would never know until he faced once more the tall fellow with the cleft chin. An odd chill was stealing through his spinal marrow, through his blood and brain. A coldness unlike anything he'd ever known before.

II

In the mind of Harrigan there remained the picture of a splendid figure, tall, graceful, strong-shouldered. The face had been masked, but there was that cleft in the chin. He would know his man, he told himself, if ever he should find him. And to follow that trail wherever it might lead, he had the hoof prints that the black horse had left upon the ground. They were big, round hoofs, newly shod. Their exact pattern he copied indelibly in his mind.

Then he drove the buckboard off the trail, unhitched his two mustangs, put on one of them a saddle carried in the back of the buckboard, salvaged some flour, bacon, and jerky, and his gear from the back. He left the wagon there. He hated to waste good property, but the buckboard could not take him where he had to go.

After this, he started on the trail of the robber.

He had not stamped and raged; he had not shaken his fist at heaven to register a vow; he had not spoken a word since his money was taken from him and his girl had left. He felt that he was overmastered by odds, but still there remained in him that strange electric tingling, that coldness along the nerves, and he could not tell whether it was the chill of fear or the coolness of an inextinguishable rage. He never had known such an emotion before.

Against all the cards of physical and perhaps of intellectual superiority that the robber held, he would balance his one strength—patience. Then, riding one mustang and leading the other, he started across country.

He was nine days on the way.

In the great flats of the Tellomac Desert he wandered in circles for two of those days, patiently, patiently cutting for sign. He found the trail, lost it in a sandstorm, spent another day of search until he rediscovered it. Among the rocks of the mountains beyond, he had a fierce struggle to keep to that trail. Hours he spent on hands and knees staring at the rocks, confused by a thousand dim signs of other horses until he had puzzled out the way the black horse had gone.

On the seventh day, his mustang put a foot into a hole in the ground and broke its leg. He was thrown on his head. When he wakened, he found that the second mustang had run away and was hopelessly lost. As for the first, he had to put a bullet through its brain.

He made a light pack of essentials, hid bridle and saddle in some brush, and went on. On horseback the thing had not been so bad. On foot, he was followed by the constant illusion of Mary Dickinson's ghost attending him, laughing ceaselessly at his foolish efforts.

He found himself once or twice murmuring answers, assuring her that, in the end, she would have to belong to him. When he came out of his sun-dazzled trance, he was rather alarmed. Men who talk to themselves, he had heard, were only a step away from insanity.

Then, on the ninth day, he came through the mountains and in the twilight saw the town of Rusty Gulch, county seat, famous during the last six months for the great mining stampede that had come storming toward it. The smoke of the evening lay over Rusty Gulch as he tramped down into it.

That was the sort of a place that a bandit might pick out to spend some of his stolen money.

How many pick strokes had gone to the earning of every one of the $10,000 of his fortune, he asked himself? He amused himself for miles, trying to compute this.

He had $3.50 in his pocket, so he could not afford to do any drinking. He bought a meal of expensive ham and eggs, then he began to go the rounds of the saloons, searching.

There was the usual crowd that appears at a mining camp. Twenty percent miners and honest businessmen, and the rest, sleek vultures. Gamblers, tinhorns, thieves, killers, all the refuse of the out trails, attracted by the magnet of the raw gold.

But these people were, to Harrigan, no more than meaningless figures composed of mist. What mattered to him was a certain pair of strong shoulders, a certain proud carriage of the head, a certain smile that even a mask could not entirely hide. And a cleft, brown chin.

In a saloon whose name he never knew, he found what he wanted. First, he saw the image in the long mirror behind the bar, a strong-faced, tall, laughing man. Then he discovered the robber himself. There was that cleft chin, that brown face, and the same smile that he had half guessed at before.

It seemed to him that he never before had seen what a man

could be. He was like a superb horse, with his lithe grace and capacity for speed. The man looked supple as a whiplash, and as strong as rigid steel. There was a fire in his eyes, in his smile. Among all those other men, he and he alone stood out.

Harrigan said to a man: "Who's the sheriff here?"

"Died yesterday, or this mornin'. I don't know who the new one is. But there's Deputy Steve Wayland, yonder." He jerked his head toward a tough-looking *hombre* with a pair of badly bowed legs and a face battered to one side.

Harrigan walked over to the deputy and said: "You see that big gent down there at the end of the bar? The one with the hat pushed back on his head? The one that's laughing?"

"Big Joe," said Wayland. "Yeah, he's easy to see."

"He robbed me of ten thousand dollars. If you'll arrest him, you'll find some of the money on him, probably, unless he's cached it."

Wayland looked with a certain amazement at Harrigan. "Who in hell d'you think I am, to try a play at Big Joe?" he demanded. He spat on the floor—close to the toes of Harrigan—and walked out of the saloon.

Harrigan understood.

He started walking slowly toward Big Joe. And with every step he took there was an increase in that cold electric current that ran up his spine into his brain and disappeared, somehow, in a continual smile that was not very good to see.

He came up behind Big Joe and said: "Joe, I'll take that money you've been holding for me."

Joe whirled about. He had a gun naked in his hand in that sudden instant, a gun that appeared to have been wished into his fingers. Then he noted the empty hands of Harrigan. He slipped the gun back into its holster. His right fist knotted. He struck up and across with his left.

The knuckles cracked just at the side of Harrigan's jaw, near the point that which communicates a shock to the base of the brain. Harrigan felt as though he had been struck with a club at the bottom of the skull. A watery weakness made his knees sag. Knocked off balance, he staggered back until his shoulders thumped against the wall.

Someone was shouting: "Steady, boys! It's only fists! Give 'em room. Somebody wants to get the taste of Big Joe. Step in, Joe . . . give him a taste of your kind of blue hell!"

Joe stepped in. He was laughing as he came. He was a big man—big, but light moving.

In Harrigan there were neither the inches nor the weight. There was merely that rubbery, enduring, Irish hardness of muscle that comes from a life of hard labor.

In him there was, also, that strange, cold electric current that ran along all his nerves and came out in his continual frozen smile. He knew nothing about using his fists, so he ran straight in at Big Joe.

A hand flashed. It struck on the side of his head and exploded a shower of sparks in his brain.

"The kid's good," said someone. "He knows how to lead with his face."

Harrigan, having been hit to a standstill, ran in again. He was hit to a standstill again, but not with one, solid punch. A shower of blows turned the trick.

Laughing, at ease, not even panting, Big Joe used the magic of that long left, twisting his fist just as it landed, so that it cut and tore Harrigan's flesh.

Iron hammers beat at the eyes of Harrigan; the left eye closed and then the right swelled almost shut. Through a red-stained darkness he kept stumbling forward.

Big Joe measured Harrigan with his left, and then used a full-arm right, slightly overhand, driving all his weight, all his power, all the whiplash speed of his striking fist into the blow. It dropped Harrigan, not backward, but slewed around, and he fell flat on his face on the rough flooring. His face struck so hard that his head bounced.

"Take him out and throw water on him!" shouted a distant voice.

"Throw him out on the street!" called another.

The flood of darkness kept pouring off the brain of Harrigan like water off a rock. He got slowly to his feet again. The laughter of Big Joe was the light that guided him. He charged in again.

"Hey! Look at the fool come in! He's a rubber man. You can't break him, Joe."

"I'll change him plenty," said Big Joe, and took a hitch step forward, shifted, and smashed Harrigan again with all his might.

Harrigan, catching at the other arm, gripped it. He felt the stunning shock of the blow, which cracked his head right back between his shoulders, but his grip on the left arm of Big Joe held him up. And, with his own left hand, he smashed home a series of short, hammering punches.

A strange cry burst from the lips of Big Joe. He tore himself away. "What's this . . . a wild man?" he shouted. And smashed Harrigan to the floor again.

But again the sea of blackness ebbed away from the dimmed brain of Harrigan, and he rose slowly to hands and knees, to his feet, and ran in toward the voice of Big Joe.

Here it was that powerful hands gripped and held him.

And he had a dim vision of a man with a wide, stubbled face, who was exclaiming: "You low-down sons! You stand around and let a kid like this get murdered, do you? Big Joe, if you want trouble, pick out a man your size. Pick out me, why don't you?"

"Lay a hand on me, Cormick," exclaimed Big Joe, panting at last, "and I'll slap enough lead into your skin to sink you! I know what you've done in the ring."

Cormick, with irresistible force, was dragging Harrigan away.

The coolness of night air poured over Jimmy. Afterward, he was pushed into a chair. Acidy things that burned more than fire were laid by Cormick on the raw face of Harrigan, searing the flesh, burning away the blood. After a time, he could see again.

And what he saw was the smoky interior of a blacksmith shop, the tools hanging along the walls and a wraith of smoke still rising from the forge. Before him stood a man of immense size and strength with blue tattooing up his bare arms. His arms hung long. His huge hands seemed almost to be even with his knees. His enormous, muscled shoulders were those of a grizzly.

"What d'you weigh, feller?" asked the man.

"A hundred and sixty," said Harrigan.

"You poor, damn' fool! Big Joe weighs two hundred."

"I don't care if he weighs a ton," said Harrigan.

"He'll lick you again, the next time . . . if you want a next time."

"I'm going to have a next time," said Harrigan.

"You are, eh?" The man grinned mirthlessly.

"I know he made a fool of me," said Harrigan calmly.

"No. Whatever he's done, he didn't make a fool of you."

"I only hit him three times."

"Yeah. Only three. But it wasn't funny, the way you hit him those three times. It was like a dead man coming to life and hitting the gent that had murdered him. Big Joe, he ain't gonna forget how you hit him those three times. Nobody else that's ever seen it ain't gonna forget the three times you socked him. How d'you feel now?"

Harrigan felt that electric current, that strange coolness of a strength flowing along all his nerves. He squinted up at Cormick with the one eye out of which he could see.

And then Harrigan smiled. The smile pulled and wrenched

and tore at the bruised muscles of his face, but, in spite of the pain it gave him, he could not help smiling still. "I feel fine," he said.

"You mean it, by God!" cried Cormick. "Listen to me, bulldog. I'll make you the middle-weight champion of the world. That's what I'll make of you."

"I want Big Joe," said Harrigan. "The hell with being middle-weight champion of the world."

III

After a while, Harrigan got up and stretched. "I'll be going along," he said.

"Where?" asked Cormick, scowling.

"To find Big Joe," answered Harrigan.

"You crazy fool," shouted Cormick, "do you want him to kill you?"

"I've got to find him," Harrigan insisted blandly.

"No, you don't. Back away from that door or I'll knock you flat."

But Harrigan did not back away. A smile puckered his face horribly and he came straight in toward Cormick.

"All right," said Cormick hastily, and backed out of the way. But he did not desert Harrigan. Instead, he followed him into the street from the blacksmith shop and went as far as the first saloon. And there he learned that Big Joe had left town.

There had, it seemed, been a fracas in the street, and Joe had taken a too large and important rôle in the fight. He had killed one man and wounded two others. Even now a posse was searching for him through the mountains.

Harrigan came out into the night air and looked at the black, forbidding peaks of the mountains.

"They'll never find Big Joe," he said.

"Sure they won't never find him," said the blacksmith. "You

147

come home with me and hit the trail of Big Joe later on. You'll hear where he is. A fellow like him can't hide himself no more than lightning. You come home with me."

"Thanks," said Harrigan.

He went home with his new friend, determined to wait until sign of Big Joe's trail had been reported on some definite point on the horizon.

He had to wait three weeks before that sign was picked up, far away.

In the meantime, he could have gone to work in the mine for high wages. Instead, he preferred to swing a fourteen-pound sledge in the blacksmith shop of Cormick. In the smoking oven of the shack, with the heat of the summer sun radiating into the dimness from the corrugated-iron roof, he worked, stripped to the waist. When he swung the sledge on white-hot bars, sparks spurted out in a gleaming spray. He was not a very intelligent workman because the thing was new to him, but his arms never grew tired. Sometimes, in the middle of an afternoon, his face was drawn and he looked sick, but he always refused to stop and rest.

"I'm training for Big Joe," he would say to Cormick.

He was the most profitable workman that Cormick had ever had, because instead of patronizing the other smithy in Rusty Gulch, men came to Cormick's place in order to stare at the man who had fought Big Joe and refused to give in. The signs of that terrible battle remained clearly visible on his face in long, ragged scars, one under his eyes, and the other across his cheek bone. The shop was filled with work that kept them busy until late every night, and that work was done at fancy prices. Cormick began to grow rich.

But no matter how late the work lasted, at the end of it Harrigan used to bring the two pairs of five-ounce boxing gloves that Cormick had last worn in the ring, and Cormick had to put them on and go half a dozen rounds.

"You don't box . . . you fight. I've got to hit you anyway," Cormick complained as he slipped here and there on gliding, expert feet, his huge fists raised, his arms a pair of vast, brown snakes, constricting, or striking out straight. "Why don't you try to learn how to box?"

"I don't want to box. I want to kill Big Joe," Harrigan said.

He refused to waste time on parries and blocking; he refused to catch striking fists in the air, as the blacksmith could do. Instead, he preferred to throw up his right shoulder when the leaping, trained hand of Cormick darted at his face. Then Harrigan would come in with both hands ready to strike, his head bobbing like a cork up and down and from side to side, as he worked to get past Cormick's skillful hands. The blacksmith, sweating, sometimes cursing, finally would have to try to hit that head away from him with all his might, but it was a hard target.

Harrigan was not clever enough to land accurate blows to the chin, but he whaled away with hooks, jabs, or lifting punches at Cormick's body just as earnestly as he swung the fourteen-pound sledge all the day long. And Cormick used to feel as though it was a sledge-hammer that was being used on his ribs.

Finally, one night, he said: "I can't keep it up. I can't work all day and fight all night. It may be fun for you, but it's hell on me. All I can do, from now on, is try to knock you out."

"That's all right," said Harrigan.

Cormick stared silently for a moment. Then he went out to get a drink.

It was the very morning after this that the driver of a freight team, who wanted a broken coupling iron welded, came to the shop with the great news.

"You heard about Big Joe? He's showed up down in Albert Creek," said the freighter.

"Has he?" said Harrigan. And he quit on the spot.

Cormick, handing over the pay, put in a fat bonus with it.

"Listen, kid," he said, "you stay on here and we'll be equal partners. You keep off the trail of Big Joe. Maybe you could stand up to him with your hands, now, but nobody on God's earth can stand up to him with guns. You keep on here with me."

Harrigan smiled. "Thanks, feller," he said. "Whether I go or stay, you're my partner. So long!"

He left at once.

He had not enough money to buy the sort of horse that he would have liked to use to race south toward Albert Creek. So he bought a tough mule, instead, and dog-trotted the poor beast night and day. Three days later he met Big Joe in Albert Creek.

It was the exact duplicate of that other meeting in Rusty Gulch. He found Joe in a crowded saloon in just the same manner. In the same way he saw the outlaw's face in the mirror. But there was this difference: when he saw himself, he did not recognize his own face easily. It looked ten years older, harder, more determined.

He went up behind Big Joe just as he had done in Rusty Gulch and used the same words: "Joe, I'll take that money you've been holding for me."

That other night in Rusty Gulch had been a rehearsal. This was the real play. In just the old manner, Big Joe whirled and slashed a fist at Harrigan. In just the same manner, the other men formed a shouting ring to see the fight.

But there was one important difference. After the first blow, Harrigan was not on the floor. That first slashing punch bounced off a raised shoulder. Then he waded in and began to drive at the ribs of Big Joe as though he swung a fourteen-pound sledge.

Joe gave straight back across the room, slamming both swift hands at Harrigan. Most of those blows glanced off, only a few hit the bobbing cork of a target that Harrigan's head offered.

The shouting spectators began to gape. They fell silent, and then a wild yell went up from one man's throat: "Joe's getting licked! Hey . . . a feller half his size . . . !"

Harrigan hardly heard the speech. As he drove the big fellow toward the wall, he could see Big Joe's body bending, growing concave, his head coming down to an easier level as Joe strove to avoid those frightful body slams.

Jimmy changed his aim and cracked an overhand left against Joe's chin. The effect was beyond belief.

Big Joe, fairly knocked from his feet, struck the wall and pitched forward on hands and knees. He fell as a cat would fall, lightly. He rose again. A gun in his right hand was spitting fire and lead.

"Wait . . . !" shouted Harrigan.

He reached for his own gun, and then his brain was knocked adrift into a sea of waves that were half red and half black, and the flying spray was golden fire.

When he could see again, and think, he discovered that there was running blood on his face.

"He's going to live, all right," said a voice that came out of distance into his consciousness. "The bullet just plowed along the skull. That's all."

It seemed to Harrigan that his head had been cracked open and was falling apart. He got to his feet as soon as the bandage had been wound about the bloody furrow.

A number of men with earnest faces stood around him. "I don't quite foller this," said the oldest of the lot. "They say that Big Joe didn't fight fair, but that ain't likely. He'll fight a Mex with a knife . . . or a Canuck . . . and he'll go with wrestling or free-for-all, or guns. Big Joe never played crooked with any man before. How come he didn't fight fair with you?"

Harrigan, looking back into the scene, remembered a certain wild gleam that he had seen in the eyes of Big Joe, and he smiled. "He fought fair," he said. "When he and I fight, anything is fair. I haven't any kick against him."

He looked about him at the others, and he kept on smiling.

IV

In the post office at the town of Albert Creek there was a large board where notices were posted. Now on the board itself there appeared, carved into the wood, the following words:

Big Joe:
  You have licked me twice. Cut out this running away and give me a third chance. I'll meet you anywhere and at any time.

Harrigan

As a matter of fact, Harrigan did not carve the letters into the wood. He merely stood with the red-stained bandage about his head and scrawled the words in large letters, using a soft-lead pencil. But such numbers of people came thronging, in after days, to read that strange and famous challenge, and so many horny fingers traced out the letters, that they began to grow dim.

Then the postmaster, who enjoyed the crowds for the sake of company, carefully cut out the wood, keeping as close as possible to the original shape of the letters. He did a very good and delicate job. When he had finished cutting away the wood in small trenches, he took a bit of red paint and painted the cuts he had made.

That was how the legend started. That is why most people

believe today that Harrigan, after he had been shot down and left for dead in Albert Creek, staggered to his feet and in his own blood wrote out the challenge.

It took some time for that legend to spread. And in Albert Creek today, the inhabitants will not deny it, because the thing that put Albert Creek on the map was the famous message written on the bulletin board in the little post office. However, the real truth is that the postmaster himself did the cutting and then painted it with red to bring it out more boldly.

But Harrigan, as he left the town on his mule, with a Winchester rifle balanced across the pommel of his saddle, knew nothing of what was to happen behind him in that town. His hope was that his challenge would be repeated far and wide across the range, through the rustling of the leaves along the dim trails, and that sooner or later he would receive word telling him that, on a certain date in a certain place, Big Joe would await him.

In the meantime, he picked up the trail and followed it as well as he could. It took him across the mountains, above timberline, and down into the broad plateau beyond. It turned and traveled east again. It brought him north into Montana, and then it turned and headed south again.

His mule was thin and so was Harrigan, by that time. But still he was following. Sometimes merely vague reports about the whereabouts of Big Joe would send him off on a week's futile search. And sometimes Harrigan followed the actual trail of the hoofs of Joe's horse.

On this occasion, he had before him on the hard soil a dim print of hoofs. He knew that the outlaw was now riding a bay gelding with black points all around. And the sign on the ground was so fresh that, when he dismounted and knelt down, he could see the ground at the edges of the impression still crumbling. A sure sign that the rider had passed that way not long before.

At last he found himself in a shallow dish of a valley, under a lowering autumn sky, and, here and there, a few outcroppings of brush. Out of one of those tufts of brush a rifle clanged. Before the sound of the gun, the bullet chugged into the body of the mule and it stumbled onto its knees. And as the mule fell to its side, Harrigan stepped clear of the body and saw a rider on a bay horse flash away down the valley.

He stood entranced, staring after the vanishing figure. The thing was there before his eyes, but it was incredible.

Big Joe had waited for him like an Indian in ambush and, after firing one murderous shot, had fled rather than remain to fight out the battle. Big Joe was afraid!

A strange little song ran through Harrigan's blood and his brain as he watched the rider fade away out of sight. Then he turned and saw a scattering of horses in the valley.

He took the bridle and saddle and rope off his mule, and after half an hour's work got the rope on the best of the horses that could find. It was a splendid gray mare, big as a stallion in the neck and shoulders. When he had saddled her and swung onto her back, he knew that he had done a detestable thing—that he had turned horse thief. But that did not matter if it would bring him any closer to Big Joe.

Tied to the forehoof of the dead mule, he had left a scrawled note that said:

Whoever owns the gray mare, I've taken her. Whatever your price is, I'll pay it when I catch up to Big Joe.

Harrigan

Then he rode on south along the trail.

He followed the sign of the hoofs until a great downpour of rain flooded the earth and half blinded him. Even so he got as far as a small scattering village and asked among the cowboys and miners in the little hotel if any of them had seen a man on a bay gelding with black points all around go through the town.

A couple of tall, heavy-shouldered cowpunchers stepped out and took the gray mare by the bridle.

"I ain't seen anybody on a bay horse with black points all around," said one of them, "but I've seen Jump Harris's gray mare many's the time, and this is it. Git out of that saddle, you damn' horse thief!"

The village was called Adobe Corner. What happened then, they still talk about in Adobe Corner.

They show you the place where the gray mare was standing. They show you the spot where Harrigan was dragged off the horse. Just beside the steps of the verandah, he actually fought himself clear of the many hands and leaped up onto the verandah.

Too many of them had felt the weight of his fists, and there was a bit of holding back. He should have reached the door of the hotel safely but Sam Walters, who had just ridden up, swung his sixty-foot rope and looped Harrigan just as he was about to duck in the front door.

Sam Walters, quick as a wink, turned his horse and started to drag Harrigan down the street.

The whole place was thundering—"Horse thief!"—by this time.

Sam Walters was a surly-faced half-breed and he was mean enough to have dragged Harrigan to death then and there, but Harrigan managed to loosen the noose and slip out of it just as he was pulled clear of the crowd.

He lurched to his feet, running, but, when the rest of the mob seemed about to spill over him, instead of trusting to his heels, he seemed to prefer to show the others his face instead of his back. He turned and fought them with his hands for five

155

mortal minutes before they could get him roped and tied. .

By then, coat and shirt had been ripped from his back. He was plastered with mud and with crimson blood welling through a thousand cuts.

Jump Harris had been found in the village and brought to the spot. He identified the gray mare and said that Lucky, which was her name, certainly had been stolen because she was the best roping horse he had, and he never would sell her so long as he lived.

That was enough for the men of Adobe Corner.

They put Harrigan on another horse, bound his hands, and led him under a cottonwood tree at the corner of the block. They strung a noose around his neck, and threw the other free end of the rope over a stout branch above.

"What you want before you do the cottonwood prance, kid?" said somebody. "You've fought good enough to earn a drink before you die."

Harrigan smiled at them through the mud. "Boys, I wish one of you would wash the mud out of my eyes."

One of the men actually brought a bucket of water that he dipped out of the long horse trough in front of the hotel. He sluiced that over Harrigan.

"Thanks, partner," said Harrigan. "I'm ready, boys."

The man raised a quirt to slap the horse on whose back Harrigan waited.

"Wait a minute," shouted Jump Harris.

The crowd turned toward Harris.

Jump yelled: "Ain't you Harrigan? Didn't I see you down in Albert Creek?"

"My name is Harrigan," he admitted.

"My God!" shouted Jump Harris, "it's Harrigan! It's the fellow who's trailing Big Joe. Hell, Harrigan, I'll *give* you the gray mare!"

"Hey, wait a minute! Shut up, Jump. That don't change him from bein' a horse thief!" yelled a man who had a swelling black eye.

"Jump, damn it, leave us have ten seconds, and then you can give the mare to a corpse," said a man who lacked front teeth.

But Jump Harris stood in his stirrups and took the noose from Harrigan's neck.

"I'll pay you for the mare, one day," said Harrigan.

"You can't pay for her!" cried Harris. "I bred her, raised her, broke her, and love her, by God! I wouldn't sell her for a million . . . but I'll *give* her to the man that can kill that murdering Big Joe."

The heart of Adobe Corner changed in a moment. From hanging Harrigan they turned him instantly into a hero. They made him stand at the bar of Sid Walker's saloon and drink, with the whole crowd laughing, cheering, yelling.

"I raised that lump on his chin," said one man.

"You lie," said another. "I gave him that just before he knocked me down."

"Harrigan, I hit you the first of all!" shouted another. "Here's my coat to make up for it."

"Harrigan, here's a brand new shirt for the punch I gave you in the ribs."

"Hey, Harrigan, this is a real Stetson. You take it along with that puffed-up nose I gave you."

"Harrigan, here's a pair of damn' fine spurs in exchange for the stranglehold I got on you."

They showered their gifts on Harrigan. He could have been outfitted afresh three times over. But he was content enough, in spite of his aching head and his bruised, battered body, when at last he rode on the gray mare, Lucky, in warm dry clothes, with a good slicker over his shoulders.

He would not stay in Adobe Corner. They wanted to keep

him there, to talk some more to them about his long trail. They pointed out that the blinding rain would make trailing impossible.

But Harrigan said: "He's riding southeast before a Northwester. If I keep on, I may wind up somewhere near him."

So he left the town and the cheering townsfolk behind him and faded away into the rain.

However, he did not reach any closer to Big Joe.

Three days later, the outlaw, who had doubled west right across the sweep of the storm, went into a store in Elk Station. He jammed a gun in the storekeeper's ribs and took the contents of the till and also a quantity of bacon, flour, coffee, and other provisions.

The storekeeper had said to him bitterly: "Why don't you stop running? Why don't you turn around and face Harrigan? Are you scared of him?"

"Afraid of that skunk?" Big Joe laughed. "No, he knows that I can't appoint a date for him without appointing one with every sheriff in the state at the same time."

V

The trail led south, at last, and Harrigan went with it as far as the last place on earth to which he could have expected it might proceed. It was the ranch of Steve Dickinson, Mary's father.

Harrigan sat his gray mare on the top of a hill and looked down through the dark of the pine trees at the ranch house beyond. He could not believe that the hoof prints that he was following actually pointed straight on toward the little log building. After a while, he left Lucky tethered to a tree and went down to examine the place.

There was not much to see of it. Axes had done the work of building, and therefore the place was small. Mud had filled the interstices between the logs. There was a woodshed and a horse shed, and then there were a few acres over which the trees had been felled, and patches of vegetables and grain were raised among the stumps. Down the other side of the mountain, sparse grazing land supported Dickinson's little herd.

The clearing grew larger as the wood was burned for fuel. And so the core of a mountain farm was growing, little by little. The tops of the old stumps were black; the tops of the new stumps were white as silver in the sunset light. And over Harrigan passed that sweet current of melancholy and happiness that comes at sight of familiar scenes from which we have been long separated.

It was not time that had parted Harrigan from the old place. It was something more than time. Big Joe had come between him and all his past. He smiled a little, a twisted, crooked smile that pulled at the skin of his face and sent a slight pain through various scars—the scars that he had received from Big Joe.

Then he went through the dusk down to the cabin. He walked with a slow step, pausing now and then. A dog rushed at him, snarling with the purposeful noise a dog makes when it means business. Harrigan stood still.

"Champ, you old fool," he said softly.

The dog began to leap up at him, whining with joy.

"Why, you sort of love me, you old wooden head," said Harrigan. He put down his hand and the big setter caught it in his teeth. Harrigan enjoyed the pain. "You damned old fool," he said. The dog stopped biting his hand. It stood back, wagging its brush of a tail so fast that it disappeared to a blur in the half light.

Then Harrigan went on to the house.

He looked through the window of the front room and saw old Dickinson stretched in a chair, reading a newspaper, with steel-bowed spectacles on his nose and a thoughtful frown on his forehead. He was still burly and strong. Men said that he was still able to shoot straight, but he had lost some of his speed of hand. Otherwise, he might have been—well, dead by hanging long before this, perhaps.

Harrigan smiled that faint smile of his and went around to the kitchen door. He was about to open the rear door when he heard the voice of Mary. He stopped. And then he would have opened the door, but he heard a man's deep voice. It was the resonant voice of Big Joe.

A revolver jumped into the hand of Harrigan. He walked around to the window. After all, this man had shot at him from ambush, and why should he not play the same game?

He stood at the kitchen window and saw Mary Dickinson washing dishes, while Big Joe dried them and laid them away in stacks on the table.

He looked fine—slim and straight as an arrow—laughing, talking there. And there were no scars on his face. Harrigan noted that. He noted, also, that Mary twisted her head and looked over her shoulder, and laughed up at Big Joe.

Joe was saying: ". . . . and so I thought, by the still look in his face that he was bluffing, and I shoved in a hundred and called him. What d'you think? He put down two pair. Queens for openers. And pair of sevens. I showed my little treys . . . the three of them . . . and pulled in the pot. And then. . . ."

Big Joe began to laugh, and the girl was laughing with him. "Hold on," she said. "It's time for you to go. You told me to let you know."

"I hate to go," said Big Joe.

"You told me that you had to."

"Yes. I have to. But I'll be back tomorrow."

"Is it safe for you to come back?" she asked.

"Meaning what?"

"Meaning Harrigan, of course."

"Damn Harrigan," said Big Joe. "I've dodged him long enough. You know why, don't you?"

"Yes. I suppose I know why. It's been a great thing you've done, keeping away from him, Joe. Simply because you know that I used to be fond of him."

"Well, you're not so fond of him now, and that frees my hands, thank God."

"Joe! Please!"

"Oh, I won't hurt him," said Big Joe. "I smashed him up a few times, all right, but that was only because he came and asked for it. But I've stood a lot from him. There's people who say that I'm afraid to stand up to him." He laughed, a free, ringing, easy sound.

The girl nodded. "I know," she said. "But please stay away from him."

"He's a thousand miles away from here," said Big Joe. He put down the dish towel and stood squarely before her. "He can't follow me fast enough. It's like your setter trotting after a wolf pack."

"I know," said the girl. "Now you hit the trail."

"I'm coming back tomorrow."

"You'd better not."

"You won't be glad to see me?"

She put up a hand and smoothed her hair. Then she laughed softly. "Of course I'll be glad," she said.

"My God," said Big Joe, "how crazy I am about you."

He put his arms around her, and she made no protest.

Harrigan grated his teeth and looked away, but still he could hear the voices.

"I love you, Mary."

"Old Joe. You'll still be talking," said the girl.

"No, only you. I never saw any other woman. I can't think about anything else. If you'd marry me. . . ."

"Hush, Joe."

"Well, will you kiss me good night?"

Harrigan heard the kiss. Afterward, he heard the rear door close, and he turned. But the footfall did not come around the corner of the house. It went in the other direction and faded out. Then he heard the dull thumping of hoofs on pine needles, the occasional clang of a shod hoof on a rock. The sounds died out.

In the kitchen, Mary was singing.

Harrigan went around to the rear door and pulled it open without noise. The girl stood at the side of the sink, her hands resting on the edge of it, her voice low as she sang the old song. Even the blue calico of her dress seemed beautiful to Harrigan. It flowed in lines of loveliness, he thought.

"Hello, Mary," he said.

She did not whirl around. Any other girl in the world would have spun about, but Mary turned slowly. "Why, Jimmy. Jimmy Harrigan," she said.

He pulled off his hat as he stepped over the threshold. "How's things?" he asked.

She, without answering, came to him and put her hands on his shoulders. He felt such pain as her hands touched him, such sharp agony deep inside him, that he was tested to the last strength of his spirit. That was why he felt himself smiling at her.

"Jimmy, what's happened to you?" she demanded.

"Nothing. What do you mean?"

"You're ten years older!"

"I'm not so old," said Harrigan. "I'm only old enough to start learning."

She dropped her hands and stood back from him.

Harrigan rolled a cigarette with brown wheat-straw papers. He lit the cigarette, still smiling at her.

"What happened to your face? What made that scar under your eye . . . and beside your chin . . . and there on the forehead, the welt that runs into your hair? Jimmy, what's happened to you?"

"Big Joe," he answered. "I owe him ten thousand dollars' worth besides all that." Then he added: "He's licked me twice, and left me for dead one of the two times. The third time will be different, I'm hoping."

"There's not going to be a third time," said the girl.

"Oh, isn't there?" asked Harrigan softly.

"Jimmy, *what* is different about you?"

"Not much. I'm the same as I always was, plus a little bit of Big Joe. Seen him lately?"

"No," she said. "Why should I be seeing him?"

"Oh, I don't know. He's been down this way."

"He may have passed by, but of course he wouldn't stop here."

"Of course he wouldn't," said Harrigan. "He wouldn't stop in at the house of old and dear friends of mine, would he?"

"No, of course he wouldn't. Why are you smiling like that, Jimmy?"

She edged farther back from him. She was a brown girl— brown, almost, as an Indian. A strange excitement had parted her lips. "Jimmy, I'd never know you," she said.

"Wouldn't you?" said Harrigan, still smiling as he blew out smoke.

"You look as though . . . Jimmy, you never must try to meet Big Joe again."

"Mustn't I?" said Harrigan.

"Jimmy, will you listen to me? Big Joe can kill a hawk in the sky with his guns."

"Can he?" said Harrigan.

"Why do you keep echoing me?"

"I'm just making sure of what you say."

"You know that what I've said is right. Jimmy, listen . . . that day when you were held up, I talked to you in a way that's made me despise myself ever since. I'm sorry. I'd go down on my knees to ask your pardon for that, if it would do any good."

"What's that got to do with anything?"

"You started to show the world, ever since that time, that you're not a coward. Oh, Jimmy, you've proved it a thousand times over. A braver man never lived. But, for God's sake, don't throw yourself away. You can't stand up to Big Joe."

"Can't I?" asked Harrigan, still smiling.

"You've tried twice. You know. . . ." Her voice stopped. "Jimmy, stop looking at me like that."

"I'm seeing a lot, and I can't help looking," said Harrigan.

"*What* are you seeing?" she asked.

A form loomed in the doorway leading toward the dining room. Dickinson was standing there, big and scowling. "Hello, Jimmy," he said. "You don't make much noise when you drop in."

"Are you through talking?" asked Harrigan.

"What you mean?"

"If you're through, go back where you found yourself, and stay there," said Harrigan.

The big man in the doorway stood straighter. His jaw thrust out and his beetling eyebrows drew down.

"Dad!" cried the girl.

"Don't worry about him," said Harrigan. "You're afraid of what he may do, but he's not afraid of himself. He's finished. There's nothing but bluff left in him."

"Get out of this house!" shouted Dickinson, flinging up an arm in command.

It was the left arm that he flung up. The right arm went to his hip, toward the weighted holster there.

Harrigan laughed. "Don't make a fool show," he said. "You won't draw a gun. Your bullying days are finished, Dickinson. I'm here saying good bye to your girl. Back up and get out of my sight." His voice changed as he spoke the last words.

Dickinson, instead of drawing back, swayed a little forward, and fire leaped into his eyes.

"Dad, will you please go!" cried Mary Dickinson.

"Yeah," said her father. "Yeah . . . I'll . . . please . . . go." He turned slowly and faded away into the blackness.

Plainly Harrigan had underrated Dickinson. He was not a bluff. He was still all man, no matter how long his gun had been idle. He was more man by the plain proof that he would withdraw from a chance to prove his manhood.

Harrigan went to the door and spoke into the emptiness of the hall. "I was wrong, Dickinson," he said. "I'm sorry, too."

"Ah, you be damned! Get through with your chatter," said Dickinson's voice from the front of the house.

Harrigan turned back to the girl. "I'm sorry I talked like that to him," he said.

Strangely enough, the girl answered: "When you were staring at me a minute ago, what were you seeing?" She spoke calmly, as though she didn't know that there was gun play imminent between that other moment and this.

"I was seeing a girl that I used to love," said Harrigan. "And, God, she looked good to me. I was seeing the old days. And the death of them."

"The death of them?" said the girl.

"Why do you try to lie to me?" Harrigan asked curiously.

"I'm not lying. How have I lied?"

"About everything. Suppose I were to tell you, now, that I loved you as much as I ever loved you. What would you have to say?"

"I'd say that it wasn't true," said Mary Dickinson.

"You'd be right," said Harrigan. "When I look at you, my heart aches like a sore tooth that's bitten down on a bone. But now I can see daylight after the sun rises. There's never been a thing in the world that I've set my mind on and then given up. But I give up you."

She had her hands in her apron as though she were drying them, they twisted so, back and forth. "I can understand that," she said.

"I'm glad," said Harrigan. "Do a last thing for me, will you? No, two last things."

"I'll do them," she said. Her face was white as the floor of Alkali Flat,

"Swear?"

"Yes. I'll swear."

"I've heard you lie and seen you lie," Harrigan said slowly, "but I'm going to believe you now, for a minute. When Big Joe comes to see you tomorrow. . . ."

She caught her breath.

"I'm not going to hang around waiting for him," said Harrigan. "I don't do what he does. I don't shoot a man from behind a bush and then run. . . ."

"He never did that!" cried the girl.

"Don't interrupt me," said Harrigan. "The truth may sound like a damned strange thing to you. I suppose it does. But if he gets a message from you, some of the yellow may fade out of him. He may come and fight it out. Tell him that I'm riding out into Alkali Flat, and I'll be on the third bend of the dry creek. No, I'll go deeper. I'll be right in the middle of Alkali Flat, on the bank of the creek, two hours after sunrise, the day after tomorrow. I'll be waiting for him."

Her pale lips formed words that made no sound. Her face, her eyes were tortured.

"You've sworn," said Harrigan.

"Yes," whispered the girl. "I've sworn."

"That's that, then," said Harrigan. He dropped his cigarette on the floor and crushed it with a turn of his foot.

"You said there were two things," said the girl.

"Let the other go."

"I've given you my promise."

"Real honorable girl, eh? Even though your mouth kissed Big Joe good night, suppose you kiss me good bye?"

She grew whiter still. But, after a silent moment, she stepped to Harrigan and raised her face to him. He put his arms about her and felt the tremor of her body. Harrigan smiled.

"It's hell on you, isn't it?" he asked.

"No," she said in a dead little voice.

"Why lie?" asked Harrigan, looking straight down into her face.

He saw her lips twitch. Her eyelashes began to shine with tears.

"My God," said Harrigan, "why do you have to act as though you give a damn?"

"I'm not acting," she said.

He put his left arm around her head so that the hard back of his hand came under her chin.

"You know what a fool I am?" said Harrigan. "Just touching you . . . but it's worth ten lifetimes to me. I'm seeing what a blockhead I am. I'm going to love you as long as I live. I'm going to love you as much as I despise your lying heart."

Then he kissed her and went out from the house. The stars were spinning in the sky, drawing out thin arcs of fire behind them. He stumbled forward, and bumped against a tree.

"Lucky!" he called to the gray mare. The quick, answering whinny of the horse drew him to her. She reached for him with her head through the dimness and nickered again. Harrigan put his arms around the sleek hardness of her neck, and remained with his head bowed for a long time.

Then he mounted and rode away into the thick of the newly fallen night.

VI

The instant the sun poured its light over the brim of the eastern mountains, Alkali Flat began to burn with a noonday heat. It kept on burning until the sun sank, and still it choked and stifled in the hot twilight dust that ascended like smoke.

In Alkali Flat there is the white, deadly heat and glare of the bottom of the bowl. Around it the mountains lift in blue curving sides to shut out the wind and keep in the heat of the sun. And that is all. It is the land of the dead, a hell hole where even the meager shade of giant cacti is unknown.

Once the bowl of Alkali Flat contained the wide, pleasant waters of a great lake, and a stream wound through the midst of it. The bed is dry now. The water has been burned away to salt. From the banks of the riverbed project roots so time-dried that they crumble under the grip of the fingers.

There was a good reason in Harrigan's mind when he named this frightful theater as the meeting place for himself and Big Joe. For he knew there was fear in the soul of Big Joe. That fear might be conquered by shame when the girl delivered the message, but Joe was not likely to risk another battle where there were spectators to witness, perhaps, his downfall. For the sake of the girl he would have to try to wipe Harrigan from the face of the earth, but not for anyone's sake was he apt to face Harrigan again before an audience.

So Harrigan waited in the exact center of Alkali Flat with the mare beside him, two big canteens of water hanging on either side of the saddle. The moment the sun rose, thirst began to work like pepper in the throat of Harrigan. It would keep on working. He could feel his skin begin to pucker and draw. Occasionally he took a small swallow of water and dampened his

himself aside and the bullet merely clipped through the muscle at the point of Harrigan's shoulder. A second shot roared in his face, but, as the revolver spoke, Harrigan whirled and threw his weight behind a long, driving blow. His knuckles slammed against the jaw bone of Big Joe. The force of the shock knocked him backward, off balance. Harrigan gripped the gun hand of the big fellow at the wrist and jammed the muzzle of his own revolver into Joe's stomach.

"And that's that," he said.

Realization emptied all but fear from Joe's eyes.

Harrigan read their frantic message. "Don't worry, even dead, you'll keep on living in the mind of Mary. That'll be a better life than you ever had before. I'm going to take your corpse back, and give you to her, Joe. That ought to be a comfort to you."

"Harrigan . . . listen to me," Big Joe said. "That ten thousand isn't all gone. I've got a good deal of cash put away, here and there. In a month I can have the whole sack of money back in your hands. Harrigan. . . ."

Harrigan laughed in his face. "What else can you offer?" he asked.

"I'll get out of the country and stay out," said Big Joe. "And I'll. . . ."

There, the cold glare of the eyes of Harrigan stopped him.

Big Joe's glance wavered helplessly away; his lips parted, trembling, the color gone from them. Then he shouted suddenly: "The water, Harrigan! It's running away!"

Harrigan, listening, distinctly heard the splash and trickling fall of running water, and, turning his head, he saw the second bullet from the gun of Big Joe had clipped through the water canteens on the right side of the gray mare and the left side of the chestnut. For a steady stream of water was running down, darkening the white ground, and instantly disappearing, drunk up greedily by the oven-hot white sand.

VII

Even with the muzzle of the gun pressed against the small of his ribs, the sight of that loss had brought the cry from the lips of Big Joe. For the loss of that water might mean a worse death.

Harrigan tore the gun from the nerveless fingers of Big Joe and stepped back, and Big Joe shouted again and made a running stride toward the horses, exclaiming: "Stop that leak, Harrigan! Stop it, or you're as dead as hell!"

But the chestnut, hearing that outcry, jerked up his head with such a sudden force that the dragging reins, on which it had stepped, snapped out short at the bit, and the half wild horse whirled and fled from its master. The gray mare followed the example as though an invisible rope tethered her to the gelding.

Big Joe, following, kept yelling: "Harrigan! Harrigan! For God's sake stop them! Don't you see . . . ?" He suddenly paused.

The two horses were racing at full speed, leaving behind them in the sunshine a double flash of falling water spray.

"Shoot, Harrigan!" screamed Big Joe. "Shoot! Shoot! We've got to stop them or we'll *never* get to water again. Half the supply's run to hell already!"

But Harrigan did not shoot. Already the pair of horses was beyond revolver range.

"We'll catch them," he said. "I'll take care of that. The gray mare's a pet of mine. But you, Big Joe, it's not water that you're going to die for the lack of."

"Blaze away and be damned, then!" shouted Big Joe in a sudden desperation. "My God, I'd beg for bullets rather than to die in the middle of Alkali Flat. It *would* come into the head of a fool like you, to stage a fight in the middle of hell. Pull the trigger and get it over with."

Harrigan deliberately raised his gun and sighted down the barrel. He took his bead on the bridge of Big Joe's nose, and smiled a little. It had been a long trail, and this was a proper ending for it. It had been a very long trail, and now Big Joe was to die.

Something else, like the gauze wing of an insect, a thin vision of a face, floated before his gun, between the muzzle and the face of Big Joe. It was Mary Dickinson. He set his teeth hard. For this more than for anything else, Big Joe was to die. And yet, if the girl loved him. . . . It seemed to Harrigan that he could see her again laugh up to the big man.

Harrigan lowered the gun. "Hell I can't murder you, Joe," he said. "Here you are." He threw at the feet of Joe the gun he had taken from him. "Fill your hand and we'll make a fresh start," said Harrigan.

But Big Joe kicked the gun away from him. "You poor fool!" he cried, pointing toward the horizon. "There's nothing but a dust cloud left of 'em, already. They're galloping all the way. If that gray mare of yours is really a pet, call her back, for God's sake. Catch her again."

"She'll probably run as far as your chestnut," said Harrigan.

"Don't say that," groaned Joe. "That fool of a chestnut will never stop till he gets to Montana. And that means . . . that means . . . ," he broke off. "Harrigan, nobody can do that . . . get out of this desert on foot, alive."

"Will you be a man, Joe? Will you pick up that gun and fight it out?"

"I'm damned if I'll touch a gun. My luck's turned against me. Besides, what good does murdering me do you? If I die this minute, you'll be dead sometime this day. There's the proof of it." He stooped, picking up from the ground what looked like a flat, white stone, and skidded it to the feet of Harrigan. It was the shoulder blade of a steer's skeleton.

There were a dozen stories of people who had started rashly across Alkali Flat without sufficient water. There were tales that made the throat and the heart ache at the same time.

Bodies had been found, always stripped to the waist, which people who go mad from thirst do—in the desert, at least. They strip to the waist, and then start digging in the ground to find water—digging until the flesh of their fingers is shredded to the bone, and bleeding. So, in a frightful, endless paroxysm, they die.

Harrigan, thinking of these things, looked back at the contorted face of Big Joe and saw that the bulk of a man was trembling with terror and with despair. Guns and all manner of battle, in fact, seemed nothing compared with the prospect of facing this torment of thirst.

Harrigan flung his own gun away. "We're going to try to march for the mountains," he said. "You go that way, and I'll go this. I ought to leave you dead here, you damn' sneaking murderer, but I've started remembering Mary Dickinson a little too well. You've got your chance. Now go and take it.

"I've been praying all these months that I could have this chance at you . . . and now I can't take it. It's as though I had hydrophobia . . . and couldn't take the drink that would keep me alive. So I'm letting you go, damn you. March off that way and I'll take this."

"D'you mean go alone, Harrigan?"

"I never want to see your face again."

"But alone . . . through Alkali Flat? That's a sure way of going crazy."

There was a perfect truth in that. One word of human speech might save a man when his brain commenced to reel.

Harrigan said: "What shall we do? The best chance is to get to the water the horses are carrying, but . . . are you sure that chestnut is a return horse?"

"He's gone seventy-five miles like a homing pigeon, running all the way."

"He'll run now, then," Harrigan said gloomily. "And the mare will stay with him. Well, Joe . . . we start for the mountains together."

"Which way?"

"Back the way we rode out. We can follow the tracks, all right."

He raised his left arm and looked at the gash that the bullet had cut through the tough muscles at the point of his shoulder. The dryness of the air had soaked up the blood, reduced it to a black smudge and a few red stains on his shirt sleeve. The bleeding had ceased, and as for the fire of the wound, it was merely an added streak of torment. One more stroke, then soon there would be a thousand lashes.

Already his throat was dry. Soon swallowing would become painful—the tongue would begin to puff—and then. . . .

He stepped straight off on the back trail with a long, easy step. Big Joe, striding out with his longer legs, was soon well in the lead, calling over his shoulder: "Hurry it up! Stretch out or I can't wait for you!"

"If you start running, you'll soon have yourself in the fire," answered Harrigan. "Do as you please and be damned. I'll take it at this rate of going."

Big Joe, as though he realized quite well the importance of this advice, promptly checked his rapid gait. He fell in at the side of Harrigan and began even then to look askance at the other, as though he felt certain that in his superior length of leg and strength of muscle there was a quality that would certainly keep him going long after the smaller man had given up.

But Harrigan gave never a glance to the big fellow beside him. His eye was for the blue of the mountains. He had lined up two distant peaks, and these would be his goal if a sandstorm wiped out the sign that they were following across the ground.

He tried to estimate their chances. One in three, perhaps, would be a good estimate. Even after they reached the slope of the mountains it would be miles before they got to the first water. And when they reached it. . . .

Abruptly he snatched his mind away from that picture. The riot it made in his blood would simply increase the pangs of the present torment.

VIII

After a time, it was Big Joe who cried out, huskily: "There's somebody coming toward us! Hey, Harrigan . . . we're saved! We're saved!"

Harrigan, halting abruptly, stared through the shimmering dance of the heat wave that flickered upward from the white surface of the flat.

"A man on foot," he said. "He won't be carrying enough water to share much with us."

"Share?" snarled Big Joe. "We'll share him . . . and the blood inside him, if he doesn't want to give us what he's got."

"What's a man doing on foot in Alkali Flat?" demanded Harrigan.

"I don't know, but there he is. A Mex, maybe. With a whole bag of water on his back. My God, Harrigan, we're going to live through it, after all."

Harrigan said nothing, but stepped on at the same regular rate. Many a mirage appears strangely in the desert, but surely not the mirage of a man slowly walking on foot.

The small shape grew out of the distance. Sometimes, by freaks of the desert illusion, the form seemed to be drifting high above the ground, with a blueness as of a lake underfoot. Sometimes it seemed to withdraw, receding rapidly. But at length it came close enough for Harrigan to exclaim: "It's not a man! It's a woman! And there's only the one in the world that would come into Alkali Flat. She's come for you, Joe. It's Mary Dickinson!"

It was she. Out of the distance, she waved her hand at them. And then she was running toward them.

"My God, she's carrying no canteen!" cried Big Joe.

She came up with a hand extended, straight to Harrigan. "You are *all* right, Jimmy?" she asked. "Joe hasn't hurt you?"

"Look at us taking a walk together for fun," said Harrigan. "Why should he want to hurt his old partner?"

She looked at his smile with a slight start and shudder. And then she saw the blackened blood that had collected down his left sleeve. "What's that?" she asked, pointing to the bloodstain.

"That's nothing," said Harrigan. "Just a little game we were playing."

She was so bewildered that she stared from one of them to the other, one hand raised to her flushed face. "Joe, what has happened? Where are your horses?"

"They ran away," said Big Joe. "And they took the water bags with them. And . . . Mary, what have you got in that canteen?"

She unbuckled it from her hip at once. "The horses . . . gone?" she whispered, and stared blankly toward the distant mountains. She understood then what she had not guessed at before.

"Here, take it," she said, offering the canteen. "I was hurrying on that poor Chatter mare of mine. And she stumbled in a regular devil's slide of rocks and . . . she smashed a foreleg when she went down. I had to finish her. I had to come on foot and all I could carry was this little canteen. . . ."

Big Joe, swishing the liquid in the canteen, groaned: "There's not a pint of water in it . . . and that's not enough to moisten one throat. We'll split it up now."

He pulled out the tin fastener lid, but here Harrigan touched his arm.

"Cork it up and give it back to her," said Harrigan.

"Harrigan," said Big Joe, "do you think that without a sip of anything we can ever . . . ?"

"Hand it back to her," said Harrigan levelly.

Big Joe, drawing in a fierce breath, stared down at Harrigan, and his glance fixed on the dry wound in the shoulder of the smaller man, as though he could see through this into a mortal weakness of which he would take advantage.

"But I want you both to share it," insisted Mary Dickinson. "I don't need so much water as you do. There's not so much of me and I don't need. . . ."

"Be still," commanded Harrigan. "Your lips are cracking already. Give her back the canteen, Joe."

Big Joe recorked the canteen and gave it to the girl.

She still protested: "Joe . . . Jimmy . . . please take it. I don't need. . . ."

"You've been running all this way on foot," answered Harrigan. "Even if you were an Apache, you'd be half dead. You *are* half dead right now. You may be all dead before we get to the blue of the mountains, yonder. Take this water, and every time you *have* to take a swallow, make it just a small sip. Wait till you're dizzy before you use it once."

"I won't touch it," said the girl. "I'll never taste it until the two of you use it with me."

"That's what you say now." Harrigan sneered. "You'll think better of that before long. Now, march ahead with me."

They stepped out, the other man falling just a little behind the pace maker. And as they walked, a wind came up—not a wind, but a stirring of hot currents that raised the stifling alkali dust into their faces, into their eyes and nostrils.

Harrigan took out his bandanna and tied it behind his head over nose and mouth. It was much harder to breathe, that way, straining the air through the cloth, but anything was better than to breathe the peppery alkaline air. Big Joe followed his example, but the girl was not carrying a handkerchief that was big enough. So Harrigan removed his own and went up to her with it.

She held out both hands in protest. "I don't want it. I'd choke under it," she said. She drew back from him.

Harrigan took her by the arm. "Listen," he said to her in a voice that the drought already had thickened, as though with alcohol, "it's bad enough to have you along, anyway . . . but it'll be hell if you make a fight every time you're told to do a thing. Stand still while I put this on you."

She stood still. Tears were rushing into her eyes, and that made Harrigan start cursing to himself softly. However, he was able to tie the bandanna around her head, and after that again he marched in the lead.

Big Joe had offered no consolation to the girl. He had not even halted, but, during the stop, he had trudged steadily ahead.

However, Harrigan was soon up with the taller man. As he went by, he glanced back at the girl and saw her stepping out manfully, though her head had fallen. Harrigan, his face covered with dry grit, his lungs burning with alkali dust, still maintained the lead.

So they went on until the rising and falling of their steps communicated itself like waves of running fire to the brain. The ground wavered. So did the mountains and the sky.

Now and then a frenzy rose in the soul of Harrigan so that he wanted to burst away at full speed, exhausting his strength, dashing madly toward the blue of the mountains. This giddiness of impulse sometimes drew him right up on his toes. But every time he forced himself back under control.

Behind him followed the double noise of the footfalls that were grinding into the dry crust of the ground. They needed a captain; he had to be their leader.

The irony of this kept his mouth twitching from time to time. He was to be the guide who led through the fire Mary Dickinson and her man—and her man was Big Joe.

Somewhere behind the impalpable blue fire of the sky there must be a mind that was aware of this, and had planned it. There was laughter among the gods as they watched that slave of duty trudge across Alkali Flat.

The mountains grew no nearer—not a step nearer. The blue had not changed. And it was the blue of distance.

He had already decided that the game was hopeless when the girl cried out: "There! Look, Jimmy! Water . . . blue water. Look! Look!"

She began to run toward the right, her arm still extending to point the way. But Harrigan leaped after her and caught her. "Steady down," he commanded. "There's no water in Alkali Flat. You know that. It's only a mirage."

She shook her head. "I know that," she murmured. "But all at once I seemed to believe . . . do you see how blue it is, Jimmy?"

"Yes," he answered, staring into her eyes. "I see how blue it is. You're going to take a drink out of that canteen, now."

"After you and Joe have had a taste," said the girl.

"You'll take a drink now," said Harrigan.

He took the canteen, uncorked it, and held it to her lips. They were as dry as paper, but her eyes defied him.

"I'll take mine last," she said. She spoke through her teeth, the challenge still in her eyes.

"I can make you," declared Harrigan.

"You won't do that," she answered tightly.

"Listen, Jimmy," said the husky voice of Big Joe, "it's all right . . . all this chivalry, but, hell, we're going to die. We're all going to die if we don't have a mouthful of water. . . ."

"All right," said Harrigan. But he winked at Joe as he passed the canteen to him.

The big man grasped it with a trembling hand, raised it to his lips. And he drank.

With incredulous eyes, Harrigan saw two swallows of wa. pass down the big throat of Joe before Harrigan's hand coulc grasp the canteen from him again.

"It was only a taste," said Big Joe. "It wasn't enough to do a man any good."

The wind had fallen away again, and their faces were unmasked by the bandannas. For an instant, Harrigan stared with a fire of contempt at the big fellow. Then he passed the canteen back to the girl.

She refused it. "After you," she said.

"All right," Harrigan conceded finally. He raised the canteen to his lips. The tepid water flowed against his parched skin. A terrible craving made his tongue tremble, the muscles of his throat work. But he lowered the canteen with the contents untasted.

"There you are," he said.

He saw her catch at the canteen and jerk it to her mouth. Hungrily he watched, prepared to see her drain off the rest of the water. But only a single swallow passed down her throat. Then she pulled the canteen away from her lips again.

IX

He corked the canteen and hooked it into his belt. The girl was staring at him.

"Jimmy," she said, "did you take a swallow or did you only pretend to?"

"Of course I took a swallow," he said. "Just one."

"I think you're lying," said the girl.

"What you think doesn't matter," said Harrigan. And he led the way forward again.

Another hour went behind them. And the mountains turned from blue to gray and brown. Victory? No, there were incred-

, cruel miles, white heat, and torturing thirst still before
em.

"Water," Big Joe begged suddenly. "Water, Harrigan! I've *got*
to have another swallow. And if. . . ."

"You've had all the swallows you get," said Harrigan. "I never
knew what 'dog' meant until I saw you, Joe."

He faced front and went on again, but a shrill cry from the
girl and a shadow that leaped across his mind made him whirl
about. And there was Big Joe with his hunting knife in his hand,
rushing at him—Big Joe with a face madly contorted.

The girl, springing in from the side, threw herself at the knees
of Big Joe. That was all that saved Harrigan. The shock spilled
Big Joe straight forward along the ground. Harrigan, putting his
foot over the wrist of the big fellow, took the knife from his
fingers. And then Big Joe rose, and the girl staggered to her feet,
also, with one hand pressed against her side.

"Are you hurt?" asked Harrigan, stepping toward her.

"Look out!" she screamed.

He wheeled about and saw Big Joe, with empty hands, but
with a face of absolute madness, leaping in at him. Harrigan
smashed out with all his might between the reach of those long
arms and hammered the blow home fully in the face of the big
man.

The shock was not delivered to such a man of steel and
rawhide as Big Joe had once been. His knees sprang under the
weight of the blow. He gave back, staggering. His arms dropped
at his sides and his head sagged over on one shoulder. He was
completely out on his feet. And Harrigan did not obey the
hungry impulse that was in him. He did not strike again.

He merely said: "The next time I'll dig a knife into you, Joe.
Pull yourself together. The rest of that water goes to the girl.
Your girl, damn you. Your girl, you dirty skunk!"

He turned and marched forward again. And the two pairs of

footfalls pursued him.

He began to hear a queer, humming sound, like that of the wind through distant wires. It was the whistle and the wheeze made by his own breathing, he discovered. When he cleared his throat, pain racked him to the pit of his stomach, and afterward he choked and stifled for a moment, head down.

The skin about his eyes was puckering, now, to such a degree that his eyes began to thrust out. At least, that was the impression he had. The skin of his cheeks seemed to be shrinking like drying rawhide, pulling back his mouth in a horrible grin.

The dry wound in his shoulder was an open mouth through which terrible flames were breathed through his body. The match was applied there, to kindle the heat that was enwrapping him.

But nothing really mattered except that his tongue was swelling like a gag that increasingly stifled him every moment. The top of it was dry and harsh as a rasp. The bigness of it filled mouth and throat. The temptation was to part his lips—but five minutes of breathing through parted lips would be ruin, he knew.

A curious and effective device came to his mind. The tongue was swollen. If it were lanced, he would be able to breathe more easily again. So he unsheathed the knife that he had taken from Big Joe and raised the point of it, very subtly as he thought, to his lips.

Suddenly his arm was caught at the elbow. It was the girl, pulling down his hand.

"Tongue . . . ," he stammered. "Thought I would . . . you know. . . ."

"Jimmy," she said, "if you go, we're all gone. Jimmy . . . give me that knife."

He gave it to her.

She stood close to him. In her face did not appear the distorion of his own or of Big Joe's. There was merely a dust over her skin and a painful look of fever about the eyes. She looked more sleepy than in torment.

She said: "Is your brain on fire, Jimmy? Rest your hand on my shoulder a minute. You're staggering, Jimmy. Tell me how you feel."

"Why, I'm all right," said Harrigan. "It's just the standing still that's hard for me."

And he walked on again, suddenly filled with shame that was hotter than Alkali Flat, for a girl had proved stronger in the pinch than he had.

He told himself that this one reproof would be enough to brace him and sustain him through anything that might follow.

And yet, in only a moment, the torture in his throat and the weakness in his body were making his feet slip in the sand. And the pain of his wounded shoulder, which had seemed a trifling thing from the first, was now multiplying. A red-hot iron was jabbing into his body there, incessantly. It was as though wasps hovered, thrusting in their poisoned stings. He could almost hear their humming, but he knew that the sound was always that of his harsh breathing.

So, keeping to the lead, watching with lowered, burning eyes the tracks through the desert, he fought his way forward, wondering how the girl sustained herself.

He was not surprised when she exclaimed, suddenly: "Jimmy . . . look!"

He whirled about, and saw Big Joe tearing the shirt from his back.

"Don't be a fool . . . Joe!" he shouted.

Big Joe said nothing. He whipped off the shirt and flung it far from him, and then he fell on his knees and began to dig at the hard surface of Alkali Flat with his bare hands, digging furiously into the ground.

Harrigan caught him by the hair of the head. "Joe, stand and be a man," he said.

Big Joe bent back his head and spat out words. They were not words. They were merely feline sounds that had no meaning. He tried to continue his digging.

Harrigan smashed right and left with the flat of his hand against the face of Big Joe, and the big man leaped suddenly to his feet. There, with his right fist poised and with fire in his eyes, he glowered for a moment at Harrigan. But Harrigan merely stooped and picked up Joe's shirt.

"Put this on before the sun begins to parboil you," he said, "and don't be a damned fool."

"What have I done?" asked Big Joe feebly. And he began to drag on the shirt.

The mountains were no longer blue. They were brown. One could see the trees like rough hair on the upturned chin of a man. One could see the glinting of individual rocks, and yet there remained incalculable miles of travel for those staggering feet. Big Joe did nothing but stagger. His brilliant strength, so famous all through the northern range country, did not seem comparable here with the powers of the more compact body of Harrigan. It was not the same sort of strength.

A cat can run fifty yards with blinding speed, but a dog will catch it in a hundred. A cat can jump three times as high as the dog of the same weight, but the dog will reach the top of the mountain first. So it was in the comparison between the two men.

Big Joe had sat too much in the saddle or at the table. Harrigan had worked with rope and hammer. All the fat had been burned out of his body; all the softness had been burned out of his mind. And he was accustomed to the burning pain of labor. Even when his body turned sick, his mind remained resolute.

There was a certain way of moving his teeth up and down,

adily, that brought a trace of moisture onto his tongue. When the moisture was there he could breathe again. When the tongue was dry, it began to swell, and Harrigan began to choke.

He had the strength. He had something else, too. The patience, which, in itself was strength. But Big Joe, that bright star among men, was a dim thing, now.

When he spoke it was to groan: "Water. Water. Harrigan, for God's sake, let me have some water . . . one sip out of that canteen. Only one sip and I'll never ask for anything else in life."

Harrigan stopped, took the canteen from his belt, but it was to the girl that he went, not to the man. "You'll take a swallow now," he said.

"I'll not," said Mary Dickinson.

Still she was not distorted. Her voice had altered a good deal. Her eyes looked more dim, more sleepy. But she was able to smile, and the chief difference was the grayness of her lips.

The delirious mind of Harrigan pondered deeply over that last change. He was not thinking very clearly or well. The fire that entered him at the shoulder was fuming up into his brain. He had to push through clouds of that fire with his will.

Whatever he thought, it seemed like a foolish, dimly remembered thing, as he said: "You're not a fool, are you? You're not going to ask me to waste breath on you, are you? God, there isn't more than one whole breath left in the world."

She only stared at him, and suddenly he knew that he had been making only an obscure mumbling noise, and that the thickness of his tongue had been getting between his teeth. There was a salt taste in his mouth. That was the savor of his own blood, and it told him that he had bitten his tongue.

Big Joe shouted in his hideous voice: "Harrigan, don't waste time on her! She's only a woman. The damned women don't count. To hell with them. There's plenty of women. You and

I . . . one swallow apiece and we can reach the mountains. . . .

Harrigan turned on him and Big Joe shrank. He feared death by torment, but he seemed to fear Harrigan still more.

Harrigan said to the girl: "Will you drink now?"

"No," she answered with unfaltering eyes.

He put the grip of his left hand on her chin. It was so small that it was hard to take a good grip on the chin bone under the smooth and soft flesh.

"Will you drink?" he asked.

"Yes," said the girl.

He put the canteen at her lips. She took one swallow and then closed her mouth. Her eyes, desperate with desire, forgot the water suddenly and stared at him.

He lowered the canteen. "You've got to drink some more," he said.

"I shall," she said. "If you'll take one swallow, Jimmy. . . ."

"My God," said Harrigan, "what a glorious girl you are. When I think that a low snake like Big Joe is going to have you . . . but I couldn't drink this water. I've got hydrophobia or something . . . and I couldn't drink this water. It's too hot. I'm going to drink about five barrels of blue water. Ice cold. Ice-cold blue water. The cold is in the blue. All cold water is blue. You take a good glass of blue water. . . ."

"*Jimmy!*" she cried.

He recovered himself. "What was I saying?" said his thick voice, which he could only know was his by the pain it cost him to move tongue and lips.

"Jimmy, you've got to take one swallow."

"If I swallow a drop, may God burn me forever in hell fire. Every drop is a drop of your life. Look . . . I love you. I hate and despise you for a rotten traitor, but I love you. You can have Big Joe. Damn him, you can have him. But . . . take another swallow and finish off the canteen."

"I won't touch it," she said.

He stood suddenly over her. "Do what I tell you," he commanded.

She became like a child under his force, and he poured the last drop of water down her throat. Then he threw the canteen away.

A wordless scream burst out from the lips of Big Joe. He rushed after the canteen, and then he stood, staggering, with the empty tin tilted up, draining into his throat the drop that was in it.

"Don't cry, you damn fool," said Harrigan to the girl. "You're crying away all the water you've drunk. You're. . . ."

"Jimmy, stop. Take hold of yourself. And Joe. . . ."

"Yeah. Sure," said Harrigan. "There's that Big Joe to think about. What would your life be without him? What's a life with one half of it broken away, anyway? I've got to drag you both through."

Big Joe had fallen to his knees. He was beginning to scratch at the ground again with broken, bleeding nails, and Harrigan pulled him to his feet by the hair of the head.

"March on, you skunk," he said.

And Big Joe marched. He did not go easily, but wavering this way and that. He let his jaw fall open, and every breath that he took was audible.

Harrigan put his shoulder against that tall, leaning figure, and pushed it forward. His legs began to ache and tremble. He found the girl beside him, helping him. They made a staggering, uncertain group, and before them arose a sheer wall.

Not a sheer wall—no, it was the height of a range of mountains that were neither blue nor brown, but ground color, with rock facets shining here and there like mirrors. Trees were no longer mere bristles. They were tall, and they cast a visible shade.

But every step was a frightful agony. Every step cost blood from the heart and the soul.

X

Up the slope lay the dead horse. The girl ran to it, at last, and came rushing, panting, back with the burden of a great canteen of water on her shoulder.

There on the verge of the slope she met them again. Big Joe lay prone on the ground, muttering and mumbling. Harrigan was saying: "Wake up and sit up, you fool. She's gone to get help. She's got light feet. Every liar has light feet. She's gone to get help for you. Stand up, damn you."

Actually Harrigan lifted the big fellow to his feet, and then the girl arrived.

It was Big Joe to whom she gave the water first.

He drank, and drank again, and again. She turned to Harrigan, but he was not there. He had turned into a crumpled heap of humanity that lay helplessly on the ground. When she took his head in the crook of her arm, it lolled helplessly back as though the neck had been broken. She tried to force his jaws apart, but they would not open.

"Water! It's water for you to drink!" she screamed at him.

"Give it to the girl," said Harrigan through his teeth. "Give it to Mary . . . and damn her for a traitor."

She put her knuckles into the bulge of his jaw muscles and forced the teeth suddenly apart. Then she made him drink. When she looked up, she saw the strangely altered face of Big Joe above her.

"He's done in," said the girl. "Will you help me, Joe?"

A quiet, steady voice answered: "I'll help you, Mary. With all my heart. Neither of us would be alive, now, except for him."

189

★ ★ ★ ★ ★

All that Harrigan knew of the hours that followed was a vagueness of pain.

When he opened his eyes, he saw rafters above him. He breathed the scent of the pine woods; he tasted in body and in soul the freshness of the high mountains.

He lifted a hand and held it before his eyes. The hand shook continually. Then he glanced aside and saw the face of Mary Dickinson.

"Hey, Mary," he said.

"Hey, Jimmy," said the girl.

"Where are we?"

She leaned over him. "You really know me, Jimmy?"

"Yeah, I'd always know you. You used to belong to me. A man doesn't forget that kind of a girl."

"Listen, Jimmy."

"Well, I'm listening."

"You see that chamois sack there on the table?"

"I see it."

"It's the money that you lost. Big Joe stole paper from you, but he's given back gold dust."

"Joe did that?"

"He helped me all the way from Alkali Flat to get you here. He helped carry you."

"Ah, did he?" said Harrigan, staring at the rafters. Then he added: "I'll be seeing white blackbirds, one day."

"You may. But you'll never see Big Joe. He's gone away."

"When does he come back for you?"

"Never?"

"Hold on, Mary."

"He says that he's leaving me for a better man than he is . . . if the better man wants me."

"What better man?"

"I'm looking at him, Jimmy."

"Wait," said Harrigan. He closed his eyes for a long moment. "I feel kind of light," he said. "I feel kind of foolish."

"Look," said the girl. "There were three dead people in Alkali Flat. None of them had a right to escape. But you made us fight through to the edge of safety. You saved Big Joe, and he swears that he hasn't been saved for nothing. He's going to start again . . . all over. Begin again, Jimmy, a new life."

"Does he say that?"

"He does."

"What a life he could make if he started it new and clean."

"I think he could," said the girl.

"He's the man for you, Mary. There's no man in the world that has the look of Big Joe, and I know it."

"I know a man with a better look," said the girl.

He stared up at her. "Who d'you mean?"

"Think, Jimmy."

"You don't mean a cowpuncher like Jimmy Harrigan?" he asked slowly.

"Ah? Is that what he is?" said the girl.

"Wait a minute," said Harrigan.

"I'll wait," said the girl.

"Give me your hand," said Harrigan. Her hand was instantly in his.

"If you mean it," said Harrigan, "just don't say anything."

A long, long silence was drawn out between them. At last he began to understand.

ABOUT THE AUTHOR

Max Brand is the best-known pen name of Frederick Faust, creator of Dr. Kildare, Destry, and many other fictional characters popular with readers and viewers worldwide. Faust wrote for a variety of audiences in many genres. His enormous output, totaling approximately thirty million words or the equivalent of five hundred thirty ordinary books, covered nearly every field: crime, fantasy, historical romance, espionage, Westerns, science fiction, adventure, animal stories, love, war, and fashionable society, big business and big medicine. Eighty motion pictures have been based on his work along with many radio and television programs. Perhaps no other author has reached more people in more different ways.

Born in Seattle in 1892, orphaned early, Faust grew up in the rural San Joaquin Valley of California. At Berkeley he became a student rebel and one-man literary movement, contributing prodigiously to all campus publications. Denied a degree because of unconventional conduct, he embarked on a series of adventures culminating in New York City where, after a period of near starvation, he received simultaneous recognition as a serious poet and successful author of fiction. Later, he traveled widely, making his home in New York, then in Florence, and finally in Los Angeles. Once the United States entered the Second World War, Faust abandoned his lucrative writing career and his work as a screenwriter to serve as a war correspondent with the infantry in Italy, despite his fifty-one years and a bad heart. He was killed during a night attack on a hilltop village held by the German army. New books based on magazine serials or unpublished manuscripts or restored versions continue to appear so that, alive or dead, he has averaged a new book every four months for seventy-five years. Beyond this, some work by him is newly reprinted every week of every year in one or another format somewhere in the world. A great deal more about this author and his work can be found in *The Max Brand Companion* (Greenwood Press, 1997) edited by Jon Tuska and Vicki Piekarski. His next Five Star Western will be *Red Hawk Trail*. His Website is www.MaxBrandOnline.com.